NASCAR

SECRETS and LEGENDS

TEAMING UP
by Abby Gaines

From the opening green flag at Daytona to the final checkered flag at Homestead, the competition will be fierce for the NASCAR Sprint Cup Series championship.

The **Grosso** family practically has engine oil in their veins. For them racing represents not just a way of life but a tradition that goes back to NASCAR's inception. Like all families, they also have a few skeletons to hide. What happens when someone peeks inside the closet becomes a matter that threatens to destroy them.

The **Murphys** have been supporting drivers in the pits for generations, despite a vendetta with the Grossos that's almost as old as NASCAR itself! But the Murphys have their own secrets... and a few indiscretions that could cost them everything.

The **Branches** are newcomers, and some would say upstarts. But as this affluent Texas family is further enmeshed in the world of NASCAR, they become just as embroiled in the intrigues on and off the track.

The **Motor Media Group** are the PR people responsible for the positive public perception of NASCAR's stars. They are the glue that repairs the damage. And more than anything, they feel the brunt of the backlash....

These NASCAR families have secrets to hide, and reputations to protect. This season will test them all.

Dear Reader,

This is my second book in the NASCAR: SECRETS AND LEGENDS series, and as they say, the plot thickens!

In *Teaming Up*, you'll meet Kim Murphy, supersmart scientist…and all-around nerd. When Kim decides she needs to take her mind off her illness by "getting a life," part of her plan is to date a jock. Jocks don't come handsomer or more charming than car chief Wade Abraham—but Kim soon discovers she's way out of her depth. And then there's the small matter of the secrets they're both keeping…

I'd love to know if you enjoy this story—please e-mail me at abby@abbygaines.com. And do visit my Web site, www.abbygaines.com, where you'll find some free short romantic stories, including a couple about NASCAR.

Sincerely

Abby Gaines

NASCAR

TEAMING UP

Abby Gaines

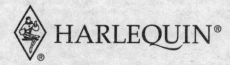

HARLEQUIN®

TORONTO • NEW YORK • LONDON
AMSTERDAM • PARIS • SYDNEY • HAMBURG
STOCKHOLM • ATHENS • TOKYO • MILAN • MADRID
PRAGUE • WARSAW • BUDAPEST • AUCKLAND

ISBN-13: 978-0-373-21793-9
ISBN-10:   0-373-21793-5

TEAMING UP

Copyright © 2008 by Harlequin Books S.A.

Abby Gaines is acknowledged as the author of this work.

NASCAR® and the NASCAR Library Collection are registered trademarks of the National Association for Stock Car Auto Racing, Inc.

www.eHarlequin.com

Printed in U.S.A.

ABBY GAINES

Like some of her favorite NASCAR drivers, Abby Gaines's first love was open-wheel dirt track racing. But the lure of NASCAR—the speed, the power, the awesome scale—proved irresistible, just as it did for those drivers. Now Abby is thrilled to be combining her love of NASCAR with her love of writing.

When she's not writing romance novels for Harlequin's officially licensed NASCAR series and for Harlequin Superromance, Abby works as editor of a speedway magazine. She lives with her husband and three children just a short drive from her favorite dirt track.

Visit Abby at www.abbygaines.com, or e-mail her, abby@abbygaines.com.

For Marsha Zinberg and Tina Colombo,
with many thanks—it's been wonderful working with you

Although Dean Grosso has refused to admit this is his last season, there is speculation that his wife, Patsy, wants him to retire. Meanwhile, it is a well-known fact that Hugo Murphy has been at odds with car chief Wade Abraham. Sources say that more than just work has Hugo on edge—and that his daughter Kim's health is weighing heavily on his mind.

CHAPTER ONE

THE HISTORY OF KIM MURPHY'S life was stored in eight cardboard boxes in the garage of her condo in Charlotte.

With an increasing sense of unreality, Kim carried the heavy boxes into her living room, one by one. She shouldn't be doing this—she *wouldn't* be, if Dr. Peterson hadn't extracted a promise that she would acknowledge somehow, if only to herself, the seriousness of her condition. "Put your affairs in order," he'd said. His other suggestion—that she tell her father the latest prognosis—wasn't going to happen.

There's nothing to tell. Because for the first time in her life, Kim had chosen not to believe scientific evidence.

"I feel as healthy as a horse," she announced out loud, as she walked from the garage to the living room for the eighth time. She propped the last box against the doorway to steady herself. As healthy as a horse that had just run the Kentucky Derby. Twice. Okay, so she was breathing a little heavily as she set the box down on the cream-colored carpet…but that wasn't unexpected for a person whose major form of exercise was lifting a cup of coffee to her mouth.

Another pleasure those darned doctors were determined to deny her.

Kim pffed her irritation as she cut through the tape sealing a carton labeled High School/Correspondence. Thankfully, she was naturally well-organized, so Dr. Peterson's little face-up-to-reality exercise wouldn't prove as cathartic as he doubtless hoped.

Why should it? She might not have a medical degree, but she was a scientist, highly respected in the field of stem cell research. She was eminently qualified to analyze data and draw her own conclusions. Which just happened to differ from the medics'.

Before she could dig into the box, the cordless phone rang on the coffee table beside her. Her father's phone number showed on the display; Kim pressed to answer.

"I've been calling since yesterday, where have you been? What did the doctor say?" Hugo Murphy's gruff manner was off-putting to people who didn't know him well. But it wasn't personal, he just didn't express his feelings—affection in particular—very well. Kim was used to having to second-guess her dad's state of mind, though even after so many years it wasn't easy.

She sat back on her heels and ignored the question as to why she hadn't returned her father's call. "Dr. Peterson said, and I'm quoting him here, 'the disease is progressing as expected.'"

"That's all?"

"Pretty much." Half the truth, anyway.

"What are you doing now? It sounds mighty quiet there." Dad always acted as if he'd rather she was having a raucous party. Of course, if she was, he'd fret about her getting overtired. His protective instincts worked 24/7, and they never took a vacation.

"I'm tidying." She figured tidiness was a learned behavior, rather than genetic, because in this regard, she took after her adoptive father.

Hugo made an approving sound, then launched into a familiar refrain. "It's time you moved in with me. You're sick, you're alone, you need company."

"But, Dad, who would look after these hundred cats?" Kim tucked the phone under her ear so she could pull a folder from the carton in front of her.

"Huh?"

She put a smile in her voice. "You make me sound like one of those old ladies with piles of garbage around the house and cats everywhere."

Hugo barked a reluctant laugh. "Dammit, Kim, would you just let me look after you?"

"No." She didn't embellish her refusal with arguments; plain speaking worked best with her dad. She flicked through the folder, then set it aside to form the basis of her discard pile. No one would want a bunch of twelfth-grade exam papers from seventeen years ago.

"I'm worried about you."

He sounded almost pleading, which disconcerted her so much that before she could think better of it, she said, "I'm worried about me, too."

Silence. Uh-oh.

"That's it, you're moving in." Hugo's voice took on the implacability that commanded instant obedience from the mechanics and over-the-wall guys at Fulcrum Racing, where he was the team's top crew chief.

"I'm worried—" she backpedaled furiously "—that I don't have a date for the silver anniversary party at work next month, and Jerry will think I'm a loser."

Her father took the bait. "You're not seeing him anymore? What happened?"

"We just…broke up," she said vaguely, aware that her colleague hadn't given her much of a reason, and she hadn't pressed him.

Hugo harumphed. "Let me guess. He couldn't handle that you're so much smarter than he is."

"Dad," she protested, "Jerry's one of the brightest guys in the lab."

But there was a kernel of truth in Hugo's words. Though Kim never talked about her genius-level IQ, her inability to speak any language other than Science Geek when she was nervous—as she invariably was on a date—didn't make for a fabulous love life. Of course, she wouldn't have the job she loved if she wasn't smart…but momentarily, her mind drifted to the advantages of cute and funny over brainy.

"It won't take five minutes to move your things in here." Hugo renewed his attack on her independence. "I could come over now."

A tiny part of her was tempted to say yes. But the minute she moved in with Dad, he'd be scrutinizing her every move, pressuring her to do things his way. As stubborn as they both were, they'd be at loggerheads in forty-eight hours. And if arguing didn't finish them off, the deterioration in her health might. She'd resolved more years ago than she could remember that she would never be a burden to her father.

"I'm too busy," she said. "My place is much nearer my office—" Booth Laboratories was on the west side of Charlotte, just ten minutes from her condo "—and I need every minute I can get in the lab. I've already cut back my hours."

"There's more to life than work."

Kim grinned. Her father devoted almost every waking hour to his job as a NASCAR crew chief. She stood, crossed her small living room to gaze out the window at the busy street below. "I also have a few social engagements coming up in this part of town."

Now that was an outright lie. But when Hugo's voice gladdened and he said, "That's nice, honey. I'm pleased you're seeing your friends," she ditched the guilt. Then he said abruptly, "I haven't heard from her."

Kim groaned inwardly. She'd steered her way through one minefield, only to be pitched into another. *Her.* Kim's mother. She said carefully, "I didn't expect you would."

"She would come back, if she knew you needed her," Hugo said stubbornly.

"I *don't* need her."

"She might be a match."

"She might not." Kim doubted Sylvie Ketchum would donate a dollar, let alone a kidney, to Kim.

"I'd give you both my kidneys, if it would do any good," Hugo said fiercely.

When he said things like that, she felt horrible for ever doubting his affection. But there was no escaping that when Sylvie left, he hadn't had a choice about looking after his adoptive daughter. And Hugo was not a man who shirked his responsibilities, no matter what his feelings.

"Thanks, Dad," she said.

"Will you be at the race this weekend?"

"You know I can never resist a trip to Indy." Kim

seldom attended the NASCAR Sprint Cup Series races, even though she loved the intense action. NASCAR was her father's world, and her cousins', and whenever she went she was reminded that she didn't fit in. She watched the races on TV, from a distance.

But she never missed a race at Indianapolis. She loved the track for its history, as well as for the roller-coaster ninety-degree turns that made both drivers and spectators feel as if the cars might plow right into the grandstands.

"If Justin wants to win, he'll have to stop driving too hard into the turns," Hugo said. Kim's cousin Justin Murphy drove the No. 448 NASCAR Sprint Cup Series car, and Hugo was his crew chief. "And Wade Abraham's going to have to stop feeding Justin ideas that don't fit with our setup."

It wasn't the first time Hugo has grumbled about Wade Abraham, Justin's new car chief. Kim hadn't met the guy, but she had a sneaking admiration for the way he'd reportedly withstood several run-ins with her father. Most men caved under Hugo's steely command.

"You tell him, Dad." Kim was smiling when she ended the call, and she finished emptying the first carton with more enthusiasm than the contents warranted.

Letters from a pen pal in New Zealand, a correspondence Kim had maintained diligently long after the letters coming the other way had ceased. A sheaf of straight-A school reports reflecting her accelerated progress through high school. She'd graduated at fifteen, moved on to Duke University. No prom photos, no pressed corsages, no love letters. She sighed, then gave herself a short, sharp shake. She'd never written a love letter so why should she regret not having received any?

Methodically, she progressed through several other boxes, all equally inoffensive.

As she worked, she was acutely aware of one carton that she'd instinctively placed a little apart from the others. The Mom Box. It held photos of herself as a toddler, then as a preschooler. Photos of Sylvie, and of Sylvie and Dad's wedding, at which Kim had been a flower girl. Kim gave the box a little shove with her foot. She didn't plan to open it.

The last three cartons held notes, folders, textbooks from her college studies. She didn't really need to go through them, but nostalgia had her opening one. She pulled out a binder of notes from her sophomore cellular biology class. This class had given her what she thought of as her calling—her fascination with the stem cells whose ability to regenerate tissue over a lifetime assured them of a vital role in treating medical conditions once deemed hopeless. The class had inspired her choice of postgraduate study, and her thesis had won her the job at prestigious Booth Laboratories.

Kim opened the binder and inspected her meticulously organized notes. In that sophomore year, she'd been seventeen going on thirty.

She flipped to the section on stem cell differentiation, the focus of her work today.

"What's this?" Her own voice startled her in the darkening room. She flicked on a lamp to examine her find. The section divider was decorated with hearts, flowers and elaborate curlicues, doodled in blue ink.

Kim grinned. Maybe not all those cellular biology

lectures had been as fascinating as she remembered. She flipped to the other side of the divider. And found a list, which didn't look as if she could have written it, except the neat handwriting was undoubtedly hers.

Ten Things to Do Before I Die

She froze.
Saliva pooled in her mouth, metallic, bitter.
The list had nothing to do with her illness, she reminded herself. It wasn't the result of some presentiment or foreboding.
If it had been, she surely wouldn't have started with something as trivial as…

1. Play hooky

She skimmed the list in search of a more meaningful ambition. The seventh item arrested her gaze.

7. Date a jock

Relief spread through her, loosening knots of tension in her neck and back, and she found herself smiling. Now she remembered. There'd been a guy, the quarterback on the college football team. Kim had admired him from afar, woven intriguing fantasies in her head.

She'd written the list after she'd realized that if he ever registered her existence, it would be as the freakish kid who'd had more A-plus grades than anyone in the college's recent history. Guys like him, she remembered thinking, dated girls who, when they weren't playing hooky, sat at the back of the lecture hall. Girls who—Kim glanced at item number two on the list—*buy a push-up bra.*

Cheeks heated, she glanced around, as if someone might be witnessing this testimony to her teenage nerdiness.

"My thirty-something nerdiness," she corrected out loud. She'd capped off her flawless attendance record at college with a dedication to her job that saw her turning up at the laboratory most weekends. Until a few months ago, she'd never taken sick leave and had to be forced to take her vacations.

Nerd!

Kim unbuttoned the top of her blouse and peered inside. She still didn't own a push-up bra. Her white cotton sports bra did nothing for her figure, and the dialysis that had added a few pounds to the rest of her over the past month possessed its own sense of irony—it had left her chest the same unimpressive size it had always been.

She turned back to the list. Maybe somewhere on here she'd find a more noble intention—like curing cancer.

3. Get a tattoo
4. Get drunk
5. Be the life and soul of a wild party
6. Drive a stock car
7. Date a jock
8. Make out at the movies
9. Dump the jock

She snickered. She'd been smart enough to suspect the jock wouldn't hold her interest for long, but arrogant enough to think he wouldn't tire of her first. She'd probably have had more chance of finding that cancer cure than getting to dump the jock.

Kim read the last item on the list.

10. Find Mom

She moved her thumb to cover the words, looked back up at those simpler goals.

Simpler? She hadn't done any of them, for Pete's sake. She'd never been to a wild party. Never dated a man who didn't wear spectacles—Kim felt an unreasonable flash of annoyance toward all male scientists who hadn't thought to invest in contact lenses.

She'd never even made out during a movie. Maybe that was because she usually went to foreign films that required her full attention to read the subtitles—and required her non-jock date to keep his glasses on for the same reason.

A thumping on her front door startled her. Oh, heck, don't say Dad had turned up to forcibly remove her to his house. Kim fumbled to do up her blouse as she headed into the hallway.

The figure she could see through the opaque glass of her front door was too slim to be Hugo. And only one other person called around here regularly.

"Where's the fire?" Kim demanded as she opened the door just in time to save her best friend Isabel Rogers from a renewed bout of thumping.

Isabel stepped inside and headed down the hallway, taking small, brisk steps in her elegant, high-heeled sandals. "I figured you'd be immersed in some horribly boring stem cell treatise." Isabel was part owner of

Fulcrum Racing, and she considered just about every-thing except NASCAR to be horribly boring. "In which case you wouldn't hear me knock. You know how you are." She took in the stack of boxes in the living room. "What's all this?"

"I'm getting rid of some old junk." Kim saw the folder with that stupid list lying open, and moved swiftly to grab it. On impulse, she tore the list free, folded it and stuffed it into the pocket of her jeans. It was a tight fit, thanks to those extra pounds she'd gained, and she fancied she could feel the folded corner of the paper digging into her, prodding her into action.

"I'm getting rid of my boring life," she blurted, surprising herself so much that she clammed up and stared at Isabel.

Isabel's beautifully shaped eyebrows rose. "It's about time. Tell me more."

Kim already wished she hadn't spoken. Maybe she could distract Isabel. "Let's have a drink. I made tea this morning." She glanced at her watch. Dialysis patients had to limit their fluid intake, but she was okay to have something now.

She poured tall glasses of iced tea, then she and Isabel sat down at the dining table, one of those round ones that folded down into a semicircle to save space when Kim ate alone. Which she almost always did.

"So, your boring life?" Isabel prompted.

The list had softened and crumpled in Kim's pocket, and she could no longer feel it. "I need to think about it some more," she hedged.

"Nonsense, you spend far too much time thinking." When Isabel used that brisk tone, Kim was reminded of the age difference between them. Isabel was fifty, but she'd never been a maternal figure in Kim's life, maybe because they'd become friends after Isabel had just suffered a series of personal losses. Ten years ago, when Kim had seen Isabel floundering and abandoned, for once in her life she'd known the right thing to say, and it had been Isabel who'd looked to Kim for support rather than the other way around.

These days, they were equals in the friendship, though the bond had been tested two months ago when, to Kim's shock, her father and Isabel, who worked together at Fulcrum, had started secretly dating. But the two women had soon fallen back into their old rapport. Kim admired Isabel's social skills, and Isabel claimed to envy Kim's self-possession, her lack of reliance on other people.

Kim wondered now if that was a polite term for "nerdy loner."

Isabel chattered on, Isabel-style, not needing much input. As Kim listened with half an ear to her friend's advice about the importance of acting rather than thinking, her fingers traced the outline of the list through her pocket.

Most of the items on it were so laughably tame that these days the average fourteen-year-old had done them. Surely it was too late for Kim to do them now? She was a mature adult, a busy scientist, with important work. She didn't have time to…how long did it take to get a tattoo, anyway? She looked at the back of her hand, envisaged a cell division diagram permanently engraved there. Or maybe a daisy.

The idea was preposterous, yet it wouldn't die. Kim took a sip of her tea, then another one. The chilled liquid seemed to seep through her body, down to her soul, reaching places that were parched from lack of living.

Isabel paused, expecting comment at last.

"You're right, I think too much," Kim said hesitantly. Then, as her resolution firmed, she added, "I need to get a life. I don't want the next thirty-three years to be as boring as the last." And there *would* be at least another thirty-three years, no matter what Dr. Peterson said.

"How did you get on at the hospital yesterday?" Isabel asked, suddenly astute. "I called your cell, but it was switched off."

She sounded like Hugo. "Did my father ask you to come by?" Kim asked, suspicion forming.

Isabel's lips flattened. "He'd have to speak to me first."

Kim grimaced her sympathy. "Is he still being cagey?" By mutual agreement they usually shied away from "girl talk" on the subject of her friend's love life. But Isabel cared a lot about Hugo and sometimes she needed to share.

"He and Justin's car chief have been exchanging words again," Isabel said. "It puts Hugo in a bad mood."

"That shouldn't affect you," Kim said.

Whatever Isabel would have said was halted by a knock on Kim's door. This time, Kim thought, it would be her father.

It wasn't.

Her cousin Rachel breezed into the condo, greeting Isabel as she plunked herself on the couch and crossed one leg over the other. She glanced at the cartons, but evidently had more important things on her mind. "Cuz, I need to talk to you."

"Did Dad send you?" Kim asked again, aware from Isabel's frown that she sounded paranoid.

Rachel shook her head. "Why would he do that?"

Rachel and her brother, Justin, had grown up with Kim—Hugo had taken them in after their father died, shortly before Kim's mother left. They were more her foster sister and brother than her cousins. But while Kim was Hugo's daughter, Rachel and Justin had always been a part of the NASCAR world. They shared Hugo's blood.

Rachel glanced at Isabel, who took the hint. She gathered the tea glasses and went to the kitchen to wash them. Kim joined Rachel on the couch.

"You know I want the new crew chief job, right?"

Kim rolled her eyes. "I'd have to be deaf and blind not to."

Ever since Fulcrum Racing had announced it was planning to run a third NASCAR Sprint Cup Series car next year, Rachel had been dropping unsubtle hints about the crew chief job to Hugo, who would recommend the appointee to Dixon Rogers, Isabel's brother and CEO of Fulcrum. But Rachel had only just been promoted to the team's engine specialist.

"Yeah, well, Hugo *is* deaf and blind, it seems," Rachel said morosely. "Every time I mention the job, he changes the subject. I know I haven't proven myself as the engine specialist, but I will. After this weekend he'll know I can handle anything."

"Dad knows you want it," Kim said.

Rachel perked up. "Did he say something?"

"Uh, no. But why wouldn't he want to give it to you?"

"Because Wade Abraham keeps acting like he owns the whole damn garage, that's why."

Wade Abraham again. "From what I hear, he and Dad don't get along," Kim said.

"They do and they don't. But Wade's hard to ignore."

"What do you think of him?" Kim asked, curious.

Rachel pulled a face. "He knows race cars. And his team respects him. But he thinks he's God's gift to women, he's bossy, and—" she was clearly saving the worst for last "—he's a pain in the butt know-it-all."

Since Rachel had accused Kim of being a know-it-all every time they'd squabbled as kids, Kim felt a twinge of sympathy for Wade Abraham. Hugo and Rachel were a formidable pair. Wade probably had to state his position forcefully, or else be ganged up on.

"Does Wade want the job?" Kim asked.

"Why wouldn't he?"

Kim shrugged. "Maybe he's unambitious."

Rachel snickered. "You haven't met him." She switched to pleading. "Will you talk to Hugo for me? Will you tell him I'm perfect for this job?"

Kim snorted. "He won't listen to what I say."

"He has a lot of respect for your opinion, even if he doesn't always show it." Rachel waved away Kim's protest. "He's always bragging about his genius daughter. He says you're the smartest person he knows, and you're going to win the Nobel Prize one day."

Kim cringed. "That's awful."

"Yeah, it is." Rachel grinned. "But I'm willing to put up with it if you'll help me out."

Kim loved when Rachel asked for her help. Deep down, she harbored a lingering envy that Rachel had more in common with Hugo than she did. The sentiment shamed her, so she welcomed times like this, when she could prove she was better than those low thoughts.

"Of course I'll help," she said. "I'll tell Dad you'll be the best darned crew chief ever."

Rachel hugged her. "Thanks." She pulled away, scrutinized Kim. "You're looking really well, by the way."

"I feel great," Kim said. *Ha! Take that, Dr. Peterson.*

Rachel stood. "You'll be at Indy, right?"

"Of course." Kim made up her mind. "And at Watkins Glen. And everywhere else." Because if she wanted to get a life, she had to get out of this condo, away from these sad boxes. Away, even, from work. The new Kim Murphy would feel at home in NASCAR.

"Cool," Rachel said.

"Cool," Kim agreed, even as her mind shrieked, *I've never been cool in my life.*

She owed it to herself to change that. Her list might be childish, but at the time she wrote it, it had been a genuine cry of need. And she'd let her younger self down by never doing those things. If she'd lightened up back then, maybe she wouldn't be such a misfit now. From now on, she would *seize the day.* The philosophy ran counter to good science, which was about hypothesizing, testing, cataloguing and eventually reaching a conclusion. Counter to Kim's whole life.

But that, she already knew, was no life at all.

CHAPTER TWO

"I DIDN'T EXPECT YOU until tonight." Hugo Murphy kissed Kim's cheek and caught her in a hug. His gentleness recognized the frailty she refused to.

Kim stepped out of the way of a mechanic pushing a trolley jack between Cargill Racing's hauler—Cargill's driver Dean Grosso was one of the favorites to win today—and the garage. The area was abuzz with activity, as teams prepared race cars for the qualifying laps that would determine the starting order for Sunday's NASCAR Sprint Cup Series race here in Indianapolis.

"I'm playing hooky," she admitted. "I flew in last night."

Hugo stared. "Good for you," he said at last.

She could have taken one of the many vacation days still owing to her, but that would have violated the spirit of hooky-playing. Instead, she'd phoned in sick this morning—right after she woke up in her hotel room feeling perfectly well. Of course, her boss had believed her and been all sympathy, which made her feel terrible.

"Did Rachel do her usual wonderful job on the engine? Good choice promoting her, Dad." She might as well get started tooting Rachel's horn. Kim looked down the line of cars in the garage. Justin's points tally

for the season to date meant his team would be somewhere in the middle. Which was a big improvement on
the early part of the season, when engine problems had
him ending several races with a DNF—Did Not
Finish—and moving further and further down the
garage hierarchy. Since Hugo had fired the team's
engine builder and promoted Rachel to the job,
everyone was a lot happier.

"Hmm." Hugo's noncommittal response was dark-
ened by a frown. "It's the driver I'm worried about.
Justin got back to his trailer pretty late last night, by all
accounts, and he hasn't showed up yet. I'm on my way
to kick him out of bed."

"Be gentle with him. You know he's not a morning
person."

Hugo chuckled. "You sound chipper. You feeling
better?"

"I'm feeling…livelier," she said. It was true. Maybe
because her presence here was a small act of rebellion,
the sun felt warmer on her bare arms, the air headier and
the clatter and clang of race car preparation resonant in
a way that riffed across her senses.

She should have played hooky years ago!

"Don't overdo it," Hugo warned. His gaze roved the
garage area. "It's pandemonium in there, maybe I
should assign one of the guys to keep an eye on you."

"No way." She could just imagine how some busy
mechanic would feel about having to play nanny.

Hugo had already turned and taken a step in the direction of the Fulcrum Racing area. Kim grabbed his
arm. "Dad, please. I've done my dialysis, I'll be fine.
Let me hang out in the garage like a normal person."

"Okay, hon, no problem." The innocent assurance in his hazel eyes didn't fool her.

She shook his arm. "I mean it, Dad. Don't you dare sneak back there and tell those guys to look out for me."

"As if I would," he blustered. "And since when do you get to tell me what to do?" When she didn't back down, he patted her hand and said ruefully, "You know me too well."

"The rumors going around about my health are bad enough," she said. "If you start telling them I need a transplant—yes, you would," she said sternly as Hugo made to protest. "It's too late to do anything about the gossip that's already out there, but I want you to promise you won't discuss my condition with anyone on the team."

Hugo pressed his lips together.

"Promise," she ordered. "Or you'll ruin my enjoyment of the race."

It was that last comment, rather than her attempt to boss him around, that swung it. Hugo sighed. "I promise. But you need to promise you'll ask for help the second you need it."

"Of course," Kim said, relieved. Once her dad gave his word, he stuck with it. She kissed his cheek. As always, he stiffened for an instant, then relaxed.

She left Hugo and strolled past the garages, enjoying the colors of the cars, the bustle of the teams. They were sensually stimulating in a way the hushed white solemnity of Booth Laboratories couldn't be. She passed the No. 483 car of Danny Cruise, saw two mechanics sharing a joke. One of them looked Kim up and down, then winked. Her instinct was to duck her head and hurry on by…instead, she smiled back at him. Because the new Kim Murphy did that kind of thing.

She glanced back over her shoulder after she passed by, saw the mechanic eyeing her bottom in her slim-fitting pants. Yep, this was where she needed to be to complete her list.

She couldn't even begin to *Be the life and soul of a wild party* at Booth Laboratories, or in any other part of her life. But here in NASCAR, no matter that everyone was deadly serious about their racing, they knew how to have a good time.

They probably had wild parties every night.

She fingered the list in her pocket—tucking it in there had emboldened her for that call to her boss this morning.

Two Fulcrum Racing team members—Kim recognized them by their orange-and-brown shirts—passed her, pushing a trolley stacked with tires toward the pits. She'd reached her destination.

The bright orange No. 448 Turn-Rite Tools car stood out from the cars either side. The hood was open, and a mechanic leaned over the engine, tinkering with goodness knows what. Kim saw thick dark hair, broad shoulders and strong hands turning a spanner. Then he looked up.

Kim's pulse skipped, her mouth dried. An aftereffect of this morning's dialysis, she told herself. Nothing to do with the fact that this guy might just be—what was Rachel's expression?—God's gift to women.

Ink-black eyes met hers, halting the progress of her gaze across hard-planed cheekbones, firm lips and a strong chin. She had never in her life noticed a man's cheekbones, she was certain. That heightened-senses-from-playing-hooky thing was working overtime.

He turned away and said to one of the mechanics, "I'm done here, give everything a wipe-down, will you?" His voice, like the low rumble of a well-tuned engine, triggered a tingle between Kim's shoulder blades.

He tucked the spanner into the pocket of his dark uniform pants, wiped his hands on a cloth and, without looking, threw it onto the war wagon with a precision that saw it land exactly atop another cloth. He'd probably played football in college, Kim thought.

More likely, he hadn't been to college. His command might have sent the mechanic scurrying to obey, but Wade Abraham—who else could he be?—possessed the kind of rough-hewn, leader-of-men authority they didn't teach in universities.

Item number seven on Kim's list popped into her mind, complete with flashing lightbulbs around it: *Date a jock.* This guy was a jock, oh, my, yes. In fact, if there was such a place as Jock Kingdom, Wade Abraham would have a pretty strong claim to the throne.

Seize the day. Buoyed by the appreciative look Danny Cruise's mechanic had given her derriere, she took a step in Wade's direction. The movement drew his glance. "Uh, hi," she said. "I'm Kim." The words were out before she remembered she was no good at talking to strangers, especially men. Now what? Her new self evaporated, leaving her old, nerdy self exposed.

Wade had no discernible interest in her butt, going by the jerk of a nod he directed at her. Then his gaze flicked to Kim's hard card, which identified her as a team member, and some of the impatience left his expression. "Wade Abraham," he said.

Kim stuck out a hand. Wade's fingers were as strong

as they looked, gripping hers in a way that sent a little shock through her. He smiled, perhaps sensing her reaction, and the slow curving of his mouth made her stomach clench.

For a crazy moment, Kim wondered if the hospital pharmacy had mixed up her meds this week, and she'd been taking some kind of female Viagra.

Because no matter what fanciful thoughts she'd had when she was seventeen, her intensely physical reaction to a jock like Wade Abraham made no sense. He was a million miles away from the academics she dated. *Good with his hands.* She felt her face flame. Then she heard herself say, "Would—would you like to grab a coffee?"

She held her breath, and it seemed to her that a silence swelled, occupying the entire space between them, threatening to smother her.

Wade took his hand back and Kim realized she'd been hanging on to him as if she'd won him at the county fair. He frowned, his eyes turning darker than ever. "I have a car to prepare for qualifying."

"I—I know that," she said. For goodness' sake, he probably thought she had a permanent stutter. And if her face turned any redder, someone would chop her up and add her to a salad. *What was I thinking?* "My father's your boss."

She'd meant to explain her understanding of the race weekend schedule, but when Wade stiffened, she realized it had sounded as if she were pulling rank.

She swallowed. "Maybe, while we have that coffee, I can talk you out of suing me for harassment."

He opened his mouth, and she'd have bet money it was to say "Go to hell."

He said, "You're buying."

Kim's knees sagged, and she put a hand to the roof of the No. 448 car. "Really?" Before he could change his mind, she sucked in a fortifying breath and said, "Follow me."

The nearest coffee was in the team hauler, but if anyone saw her there with Wade, she'd be paralyzed with embarrassment. Instead, she hastened toward the coffee stand just outside the garage area. She didn't look over her shoulder to see if he was behind her. She didn't need to—she sensed his gimlet gaze on her shoulder blades.

She pulled her purse out of her bag. "What will you have?" At last, she dared to look at him. And found him standing so close that her skin prickled.

"A double espresso, thanks."

She ordered the same, and a couple of minutes later they were heading with their paper cups to a standing bar.

Kim sipped her coffee and realized that in her flustered state she'd forgotten to add sweetener. She grimaced.

"SOMETHING WRONG?" WADE ASKED. Kim Murphy's face was incredibly expressive. Maybe it was the fairness of her skin and the ease with which she blushed, but it seemed as if every thought, every emotion, paraded across her countenance.

She shook her head. "I'm fine." But she flicked a betraying glance at the coffee cart.

"Sugar?" he said.

She blushed again. "I do usually…but I'm okay without it."

He strode back to the cart, grabbed a couple of sachets and a stirrer.

Kim fumbled the sachet as she tipped sugar into her coffee. Why the heck was she so nervous?

Her comment about her father being his boss had hit a sore spot, but Wade had soon realized she wasn't pulling rank. Then she'd made him smile, which reminded him the sun was shining and although he was busy, it was good to take time out. He hadn't done enough of that.

He eyed his coffee date. She was pretty, with a classic bone structure that promised her looks wouldn't fade with time. Honey-blond hair fell straight to her shoulders—she'd pushed it back behind her ears, an unsophisticated style.

She took another sip of her coffee, eyeing him warily. For someone who'd been so keen to have coffee with him, she didn't have much to say. Wade glanced at his watch. He'd need to wrap this up in a few minutes, get back to the car. He made an attempt at conversation. "Do you work for the team?"

She started. "No, I'm a scientist."

Man, she was jumpy. There'd been a flash of chemistry between them when they shook hands—Wade had dismissed it, but it seemed she hadn't. Now, her hyperawareness of him was having the same effect on Wade. He had to force himself to keep his eyes on her face. He'd checked out her figure as she ordered the coffees and found curves that were rounded enough to be just to his taste, and great legs that deserved another look.

"Sport science?" he guessed.

"Stem cell research. Stem cells are—well, they're sort of starter cells that can turn into other kinds of cells." She peered at Wade as if uncertain that he understood. "If we can differentiate—by which I mean *transform*—those starter cells into, uh, specialized cells, such as for various body tissues, then we can…" She trailed off and said apologetically, "It's pretty complicated."

He agreed, thinking of the popular science magazine to which he subscribed. "Do you work with embryonic or adult cells?" he asked. Because he could, not because he was interested in the answer.

Her gray eyes widened. "Uh, adult cells. Do you know something about stem cell research?"

"Something. How come I haven't seen you at the track before?"

"I HAVEN'T HAD much spare time this season." Kim's stomach was fluttering like a butterfly on speed and she had the craziest urge to confide in Wade. To confess that even when she came to the races she seldom entered the garage because she always felt so out of place. *Gee, that'll surprise him.*

"No time, huh? Stem cells dividing too fast?"

About to clarify the speed at which stem cells divided, she realized he was teasing. "Um, I hope to make it to every race from now on," she said. If he felt the same attraction she did, this was his opportunity to suggest seeing her again.

Wade didn't take it. What had she thought? That while she'd been unearthing her list, he had been moping in his apartment somewhere, despairing that he'd ever meet a woman who'd offer him intellectual stimulation? She swallowed a hiccup of panicky laughter. This was her challenge, not his, and she knew what she had to do next.

Perspiration slid down Kim's back. Standing next to

Wade, meeting his dark eyes, knowing that if she reached out just a few inches she'd make contact with his strong, tanned forearm…it was sensory overload. With her free hand, she gripped the edge of the standing bar, before she went under for the third time. She'd never been so out of depth in her life.

"Would you like to have dinner with me sometime?" she blurted. Then realized he'd probably like nothing less. "I mean, *will* you have dinner with me?" A pause. "Maybe after a race?" He might think she meant tonight—but she'd need a lot more time to mentally prepare for a date with this jock. She added, "Soon?"

At last she shut up. Good grief, she'd asked the question in more fits and starts than a misfiring carburetor. She'd be lucky if he'd remembered what it was about by the time she got to the end.

Wade's brows drew together. "You're asking me on a date?"

It seemed he got the gist, after all. "Yes." Now that it was out in the open, Kim felt better.

His dark eyes examined her. "You think we have much in common?"

"I have no idea," she lied. She knew for sure they had nothing in common.

"Then why did you ask?"

She glared at him. She'd wanted to seize the day, she hadn't banked on having to wrestle it to the ground and subdue it by force.

With a vague motion of her hand she said, "Why does a woman usually ask a man to dinner?"

He thought about that. "Because she has the hots for him?"

Darn, she'd walked right into that one. "I'm sure there are other reasons," she said feebly.

Wade chuckled, and the flash of white teeth, the sudden easing of his broad shoulders, made him much more approachable. Three girls walking by on the other side of the fence directed appreciative looks at him. One of them uttered a catcall and he grinned, waved lazily. With their bare midriffs, perfect tans and flicky blond hair, they looked like an ad for sunscreen. By comparison, Kim felt pale and uninteresting.

She mustered her waning determination, cleared her throat and got his attention back. Which was a miracle in itself, given the competition. Unjustifiably heartened, she said curiously, "I suppose you get invited out all the time. By—" she nodded toward the girls "—women like that."

His look was quizzical. "Sometimes. Normally I prefer to do the asking." One of the girls blew him a smoochy kiss, and he flashed her a thumbs-up without really looking at her.

"You did that automatically," Kim said, half to herself. "It wasn't a sign of particular interest on your part at all." She wondered if the same went for the wolf whistle the crew guy in the garage had given her. "It's a kind of modern dating-mating ritual," she said thoughtfully. She needed to learn to distinguish genuine attraction from instinct, if she was to have any luck finding a jock to date.

Wade frowned. "What are you talking about?"

"The thumbs-up you gave that girl when she blew a kiss."

"I didn't—" He stopped. "Did I?"

"Definitely instinctive rather than intentional," she decided. "I'm no sociologist, but I imagine those instinctual gestures have been around since Neanderthal times."

Wade sputtered then choked on his coffee. Which had the surprisingly satisfying result of sending the girls into a fit of giggles. Kim patted him on the back, trying to ignore the play of firm muscle beneath her touch. The girls wandered away.

"Ouch," Wade said, to a particularly hard thump on his back. "Give it up, I'm fine." He set his cup down on the bar, scowled at her. "So who exactly are you calling Neanderthal?"

Darn, she'd just made things even worse.

Then he said, "So, this dinner…" and her hopes spiked sky-high.

"If I refuse," he said, "will you complain to your father?"

And just like that, Kim's humiliation was complete. "I, um, I have to go," she muttered, head down so he wouldn't discern the tears pricking at her eyelids. She tossed her empty cup at the nearest trash can. It fell short, so she had to stoop and pick it up.

She hurried toward the infield tunnel. Isabel would be in the sponsor suite, so Kim could hide out with her while she watched the race. While she gave the new Kim Murphy a serious pep talk. Because, mortifying though her encounter with Wade had been, she wasn't about to give up on getting a life.

Though next time she asked a jock for date, she'd choose one at least a dozen levels below Wade on the jock hierarchy. That way, she might stand a chance.

Of course, she might need to improve her technique.

She'd threatened Wade with her father, she'd insulted his intelligence and she'd called him a Neanderthal. She didn't read *Cosmopolitan,* but she was pretty sure none of those tactics would make a list of *Top Ten Ways to Get Him to Say Yes.*

CHAPTER THREE

WADE WATCHED KIM LEAVE, his attention held by her curvy behind in her black pants. There was something intriguing about her—if she'd been more relaxed and less inclined to put his every move under the microscope, he might have taken her up on that dinner invitation.

"Wade," Hugo called from behind him.

Wade dragged his eyes away from his boss's daughter's rear. He waited for Hugo to catch up.

"Justin's worried the car will push into the turns the way it did at Chicago," Hugo said. "We need to stiffen the right rear shock some more."

"Already done," Wade said. "I figured Justin would come back with that."

The older man frowned. "You should have talked to me."

Wade might have known that rather than being pleased the car was set up right, Hugo would worry about process. It was frustrating for someone as independent as Wade. Sure, as crew chief, Hugo had overall responsibility for the car. But he was also responsible for race strategy, pit strategy and driver communication. That was why the crew chief delegated to the car chief—Wade—the job of getting the car into the best possible shape to win the race.

Wade and Hugo typically had a discussion about setup when they got to the track, and they would confer at various stages over the weekend. But most of the time, Wade worked on instinct, rather than a blueprint laid down by his boss. He demanded the best of his team, and the guys delivered. In his opinion, Hugo should let them get on with it.

When he'd joined Fulcrum at the beginning of the season, he'd figured that if he did a brilliant job with the car and ran his team well, Dixon Rogers would have to consider him for the job of crew chief on Fulcrum Racing's third NASCAR Sprint Cup Series car.

Turned out it was a whole lot more complicated.

Hugo Murphy was the one who would make the recommendation on the new crew chief to Dixon. And Wade now knew what everyone else did—that when Hugo put his weight behind something, Dixon didn't argue.

Wade and Hugo had butted heads from day one. Wade had been a crew chief in the NASCAR Craftsman Truck Series a couple of years ago, where he'd had all the autonomy he needed. But he'd always had his eye on the NASCAR Sprint Cup Series, the pinnacle of motor racing, and when his family commitments eased off enough to allow him to take on the challenge of a NASCAR Sprint Cup job, he'd made his move. Of course, he hadn't been able to step in at crew chief level—those positions were scarce and jealously guarded.

So he'd spent two years as a mechanic for Cargill Motors, and now he was car chief here at Fulcrum. Most days, Wade couldn't figure out why Hugo had hired him.

But he wouldn't give up on that crew chief job.

With that in mind, he kept his tone semiconciliatory. "Anything else you want to know?"

"I want to know what you were doing with my daughter," Hugo said.

Great. Another black mark against Wade to add to Hugo's lengthening list.

"We had coffee," Wade said discouragingly.

Hugo's eyes narrowed. "Kim broke up with someone recently and she doesn't need—"

"Coffee was her idea," Wade interrupted.

"*Her* idea?" Hugo's disbelief turned to mild surprise under Wade's steady gaze. He scratched his head. "Did she say anything?"

Wade shot him a querying look.

Hugo harumphed. "About how she is. Her health."

"Nothing. Is something wrong?" Kim had looked fine, maybe a little tired.

Hugo started to speak, then clammed up. With an impatient wave of a hand, he started again. "She has some kidney problems—lots of people know that," he told Wade with an odd belligerence.

Wade gave a noncommittal nod.

"She keeps telling me she's fine, says she hasn't got worse, but there's not a damned thing I can do to find out if it's true." The bitter rush of words was more than Wade had heard Hugo say in one burst.

Hugo stopped walking, forcing Wade to do the same. "I asked her doctor, but he said he 'couldn't breach patient confidentiality.'" The mincing tone Hugo used to report the doctor's words expressed contempt for medical ethics, at least where his daughter was concerned.

"Maybe she said she's fine because she *is* fine." Wade felt a flash of sympathy for Kim. When Hugo got a bee in his bonnet about something, he was hard to deter.

Hugo scowled. "She thinks I believed her, but I can tell something's wrong. She's as stubborn as a stuck lug nut, and about as talkative. If I keep asking, she'll clam up even tighter." He resumed his stride toward the garage. "You plan to see her again?"

Kim's dinner invitation flitted through Wade's mind. He hadn't actually replied to it before she left. "Is that any of your business?"

"Maybe." Hugo glanced around, then leaned into Wade. "I'd like you to do something for me. Take her out, see if you can get her to tell you what the doctor said."

Wade stared. When it came to family, he had a mile-wide protective streak himself. But Hugo was out of line.

"Are you asking me to date your daughter," he said, "or to spy on her?"

A red flush spread along Hugo's jaw. "Neither," he said testily, then added, "Both."

"Forget it."

Hugo's chin jutted. "I wouldn't ask if I didn't think it was necessary."

"Just how sick do you think she is?" Overhead, the sun passed behind a cloud, leaving Wade suddenly cold.

Hugo hesitated. "That's what I want to know." His gaze slid toward the Fulcrum Racing garage, which they were fast approaching. He slowed down. "I'm her father, the only parent she has right now. If she won't tell me the truth, I'll have to find out some other way."

"If she's ill, she's not likely to tell me."

"You're not the one she's worried about upsetting,"

Hugo said. "And she knows you and I—" he rammed his hands into his pockets "—don't always get along, so she'll assume you won't tattle to me."

"Given you don't like me—" Wade believed in calling a spanner a spanner "—I'm surprised you want me to date your daughter."

Hugo's mouth tightened. "I like you just fine, and she liked you enough to ask you for coffee. She's lonely and, hell, even I can see you're a good-looking son of a gun. That might get you through a couple of dates, but believe me, you're not her type."

Wade was getting sick of the Murphy family casting aspersions on his intellect. "You mean, I'm not smart enough?"

"No one's smart enough." Hugo's voice held a mixture of pride and awe. "But, yeah, she goes for scientists and the like." His expression turned contemplative, as if he was recalling a parade of PhDs through Kim's life. Wade quelled a twinge of irritation. "Boring, most of 'em," Hugo concluded. "I invited one of them to a race and he didn't know a stock car from a bicycle."

They fell into a perplexed, almost companionable silence as they tried to imagine the appeal of a guy who couldn't talk NASCAR.

"Look, Wade," Hugo said, "I've seen you chatting to the girls who come through the garage, and it seems you can be charming when it suits. All I ask is that you turn some of that charm on Kim just long enough to find out how she's doing. It would help me sleep at night."

Wade knew how it felt, to worry so much that you lay awake all night. He didn't plan ever to do it again.

Now, he saw the lines of fatigue around Hugo's eyes, the strain etched into his forehead. He wouldn't wish that kind of worry on anyone.

He reminded himself that dinner had been Kim's idea. She *wanted* to go out with him. So maybe it wasn't such a big deal.

He said, "I'll take her to dinner, see what I can learn."

"That's great." Hugo's face brightened. "Oh, and she needs a date to her company's anniversary party, too."

"One dinner," Wade said deliberately. "That's all. And I can't do it this weekend because I have family commitments." He already felt guilty about giving his family less time than he used to. He wasn't going to disappoint them when they'd traveled all the way to Indy.

Hugo checked his watch, as if Wade was threatening to walk off the job before the race even started. "Call her Monday, then."

"Unless you want her to figure out you're interfering, it's best to wait until next weekend's race," Wade said. "More natural."

Eventually, Hugo nodded. "She's not going to Pocono. Try Watkins Glen. But if you're going to wait that long, you'd better be prepared to work fast. To be extra charming." It was almost a joke from the dour crew chief. But the levity didn't last—his brows drew together in a frown. "You realize this doesn't have any impact on my recommendation for the new crew chief role."

"Right." But Wade didn't believe it. Maybe Hugo wouldn't intentionally let Wade's willingness to help him influence his decision. But family meant a lot to him.

Justin Murphy was more like Hugo's foster son than a nephew, and right now Justin's sister, Rachel, was the front-runner for the crew chief job, even though Wade considered himself far better qualified. No matter what Hugo liked to think about his impartiality, family mattered at Fulcrum Racing.

With Dixon Rogers planning to announce the new crew chief at the Richmond race in September, there wasn't much time for Wade to overcome the man's prejudices. Some days he felt as if he was singlehandedly pushing a stock car uphill. Doing Hugo a favor might help change that.

The more Wade thought about it, the more the idea of dinner with the probably perfectly healthy Kim Murphy seemed a win-win situation. Kim would get the date she wanted, Hugo would have the reassurance he needed and Wade might just score a chance to build a bridge with his boss that would stretch all the way to the crew chief job.

WADE DIDN'T REALIZE how much Kim had occupied his mind until he saw her on practice day ahead of the race at Watkins Glen. He was overseeing the changes the guys were making to the car between practice laps, when just the first glimpse of Kim's honey hair on the other side of the pit wall brought every feature of her face into sharp focus in his mind.

He returned his concentration to the trackbar adjustment being made to the race car, but through his usual intensity he heard Kim's low voice as she talked to her father, far more confident than when she'd stammered her dinner invitation last week. Once, a laugh traveled across the stacks of tires between them, and it had the odd effect of lifting the hairs on Wade's arms.

He glanced in her direction a couple of times, looking for an opportunity to tell Kim he would accept her invitation. The fondness on Hugo's face was remarkable for a man who was sometimes distant, mostly gruff, always demanding. He and Kim obviously got along well, despite Hugo's overprotectiveness.

When Hugo went to brief Justin in the hauler, Wade approached Kim. He took in the prim chic of her pinstripe blouse, the jeans that lengthened her legs enticingly. Taking her on a date wouldn't be a hardship.

"I didn't get to answer your dinner invitation back in Indy," he said.

KIM HAD SPENT THE week wondering if there was any way she could see Wade without feeling like an idiot. In the end, she'd decided she would ask a couple of questions about Justin's car setup, wish him luck and walk away as if she'd never done anything so rash as to ask him on a date. But as soon as he spoke, the calm, polite conversation she'd rehearsed went right out of her head. She had a bad case of teenage girl syndrome and, like chicken pox, it was far more severe when contracted in adulthood.

As she groped for words, she tried not to notice that his biceps were beautifully sculpted, his shoulders powerful in his team T-shirt. *Pesky jock.* With an inward sigh, she ditched her questions about shock absorbers and tire pressure, and decided the best she could hope for was that she wouldn't make a fool of herself this time. "No need," she said. "I withdraw the offer." That would save them both some embarrassment.

He eyed her for several long, silent seconds. Kim was good at silence, so she eyed him back. He broke first.

"Then I'll invite you," he said. "How about dinner after the race tomorrow?"

Was this a joke? His lips were a straight, unsmiling line. Kim's pulse thudded at the thought he might have meant it. Then she remembered. "I'm going to the sponsor party," she said, relieved. Justin's primary sponsor, Turn-Rite Tools, was hosting a corporate hospitality event, and they wanted as many of the team as possible there to rub shoulders with their clients and company bigwigs. Hugo had insisted Kim come along, too, so she could "get out of herself."

"Yeah, me, too." Wade took her elbow to tug her out of the way of a team member pushing a trolley jack. "But we'll go to dinner afterward."

He couldn't possibly be interested in her, not when he had gorgeous, tanned girls after him. Unless, of course, he was one of those jocks whose head hurt when a woman talked too much. In which case Kim's tongue-tied behavior might have been a turn-on. She pondered the likelihood.

She should accept his offer. After all, she had a goal of dating a jock. But Wade was out of her league. No need to make this any harder on herself than it had to be.

"Thanks," she said, "but I have work to do."

His knowing look accused her of a cop-out, and she felt obliged to explain. "When I feel as if I'm close to a breakthrough, every hour away from my laptop is like a physical ache."

Why didn't she just tattoo Supernerd on her forehead, and cross item number three off her list?

To her surprise, Wade nodded. "I feel like that when I'm away from the workshop and it suddenly hits me how we can get the car cornering better. I want to drop everything and get to it."

"Exactly." She beamed at him. Hugo brushed past her to climb the pit box, directing a curious glance her way.

"So, what kind of breakthrough are you talking about?" Wade asked.

"Oh, ah, you wouldn't—" She caught the sharp intelligence in his eyes, and backpedaled. She'd already insulted him enough for one lifetime. "Recent studies have indicated that we might be able to reprogram adult stem cells so they take on some of the qualities of embryonic stem cells, without actually having to use embryonic cells."

He appeared to still be with her.

"But no one's figured out how to do the reprogramming in a way that won't harm humans," she said. "At the moment it requires an oncogene, which can cause cancer."

"And you think you can figure out a better way?"

She shrugged. "Someone can. Maybe I'm that someone."

He watched her through hooded eyes. "I asked a couple of the guys about you. Everyone says you're incredibly smart." His mouth quirked. "In fact, one of the tire guys is convinced you've won a Nobel Prize."

Kim groaned. "Of course I didn't."

He hooked his thumbs in the pockets of his pants. "But you're some kind of genius, right?"

"It's just a number," she muttered, red-faced. Wait 'til she got a hold of Dad!

"You make it sound like a bad thing." He sounded puzzled.

She made a dismissive noise.

"You shouldn't be ashamed of who you are," he said.

Who she was was exactly what she wanted to change. "I'm not ashamed," she said, "but if people think you're even capable of winning the Nobel Prize, they can get…intimidated."

"So that's why you won't go to dinner with me? To spare me the intimidation?"

"You're twisting my words."

"Do you date guys who don't have PhDs?"

She wasn't sure if he was teasing or not. "I would," she said cautiously.

"But no one's asked you?" he said, incredulous.

She shook her head.

Wade stepped closer, imposing his rugged masculinity on her personal space. "Here's a thought—how about we take it as a given that you're smarter than I am, and that I don't give a damn?"

Kim shivered. Every man she'd ever met gave a damn about her intelligence. Whether it baffled them, as it did her father, impressed them—her college professors—intimidated them, or just plain ticked them off.

Now she was the one who was baffled and intimidated. "You weren't exactly hanging out to date me last week. What's changed?"

Two women—fans with cold passes, she guessed—walked past them. One of them, a pretty redhead, grabbed her friend's arm, said something in an excited undertone, then headed for Wade.

"You're Wade Abraham, Justin's car chief," she said. "I saw your interview on TV last week."

Justin had won the race in Indianapolis, so Rachel

and Wade had ended up fielding a few questions on a major network sports show. Kim had told herself not to watch, but left her finger hovering over the remote's off button until the interview ended.

"Yep, that's me." Wade shook hands with the fan and her friend, gave them a smile that could only be described as a ladykiller.

"You were so cool, the way you could translate all those numbers into performance predictions," the redhead said. She inched closer to Wade. "Your job must be fascinating."

Huh, so that's how you talk to a jock.

Wade's smile widened. It didn't take a rocket scientist to figure out where this was headed.

"I'd love to hear more about it," the woman cooed. "What say we meet for a drink tonight?"

"I don't drink the night before a race." He sounded regretful, and Kim wondered if it was true.

"How about after the race?" the woman persisted.

Wade's dark gaze flickered in Kim's direction, as if inviting her to stake a claim on him. She took a step backward. Far from looking disappointed, he bit down on a laugh.

"I have a sponsor party after the race," he said, "then a dinner date."

The heck he did. Alarmed, Kim said, "I'm sure your date won't hold you to it."

The women glanced her way, curious.

"I wouldn't bet on it," Wade said. "She seems pretty keen."

"I—I suspect you're misreading the situation," Kim managed to respond.

He shook his head, and his warm gaze heated her skin. Her mind buzzed with the unfamiliar stimulation.

"Well, goodbye." The redhead moved off.

Wade grinned at Kim, and it literally stole her breath away. "So, we're on for dinner?" he asked.

This man is dangerous. She sucked in some air. "I'm sorry," she said. "I shouldn't have used all those big words. Let's try again with one syllable—no."

To her chagrin, Wade threw back his head and laughed.

WHEN JUSTIN MURPHY SLIPPED back a couple of places during the second half of Sunday's race, Hugo ordered the No. 448 car to be tightened up during the pit stop. Wade felt the decision was driven more by the fact that Dean Grosso's car was noticeably tighter than Justin's, than by Justin's needs. Although Hugo would probably deny he felt any real animosity toward Dean or his family these days—especially now that Justin was dating Sophia Grosso—the long-standing family feud between the Murphys and the Grossos meant both families hated to see someone from the other side leading a race. As Dean was right now.

Wade climbed the ladder up to the war wagon, where Hugo was watching Justin's progress on the screen. It was impossible to see the car everywhere on the two-and-a-half-mile road track, whose hills and *S* curves made it one of the most interesting NASCAR venues for both fans and drivers.

"The car's too tight," he told Hugo.

Hugo grunted, shook his head without looking up.

"Justin's having trouble getting the front out of the corners," Wade said.

"That's because he needs new tires. Everybody else has been tightening up the whole way through."

"We need to put in a rubber," Wade continued, convinced that inserting a rubber block between two coils of the right rear spring would loosen the car up just right.

Hugo leaned close to the screen to watch Justin in one of the *S* turns.

"It's possible that it's too tight," he conceded. "But Justin said it's loose."

"That's his cornering, not the car," Wade said bluntly. "Our setup isn't producing the result we want. I say we change it." He pushed his point home. "Justin has five more laps before he pits. If he hasn't picked up a place by then, I want to try a rubber."

"It'll slow the pit stop," Hugo said.

"We'll have him out of here in fourteen, I promise." The promise was a risk—fourteen seconds wasn't much time to do all the things Justin needed.

"You'd better."

It took a second for Wade to realize Hugo had given in. The older man didn't look happy. Without taking his eyes off the screen, he said, "You talk to Kim yet?"

Wade's sense of victory faded. "I asked her to dinner tonight. She turned me down."

Hugo looked torn between irritation and satisfaction that Kim had found Wade so resistible. "I need to know how she is," he said. "What's your plan?"

"My plan is to get Justin's car right, so we have a shot at winning this race."

He meant it, Wade thought, as he climbed down off the war wagon to brief the guys on the imminent pit stop. This dinner with Kim was turning complicated, and he couldn't afford the distraction. If he didn't get the car right, Hugo wouldn't rate him for the crew chief job. He just hoped the same thing wouldn't apply if he failed to convince Kim to go to dinner.

The sooner Wade got Kim to dinner and persuaded her to part with the information Hugo wanted, the better.

CHAPTER FOUR

JUSTIN FINISHED SECOND, a whisker behind Danny Cruise—an incredible result given his struggles halfway through the race, which the pundits were already labeling one of the year's most exciting.

So Kim couldn't blame the lack of her usual enjoyment on the race itself. She'd taken a position on the corner at the bottom of the hill, only to find that although her gaze stayed fixed on the cars, her mind wandered with a shocking lack of discipline.

Not too far, though. Just as far as Justin's car chief. Was her life so dull that she got fixated on the first jock who smiled at her?

After the race, she returned to Justin's motor home for her dialysis, then got ready for the Turn-Rite Tools party. Her pale blue silk dress was robbed of sophistication by its sweetheart neckline, but the above-the-knee skirt made her legs look good, and the color suited her.

As Kim walked into the Fulcrum Racing sponsor suite, she wondered if this would be a wild party. She didn't regret turning Wade down—in fact, she was quite pleased with herself for holding her ground, when the man was obviously used to women falling at his feet—but she was aware she needed to make progress with her list.

She surveyed the room, full of people happy their driver had done so well. Instinctively she looked for Wade. She didn't find him—which did *not* disappoint her.

"You're here." Isabel stated the obvious as she kissed Kim's cheek.

"Looks like a good party." Though Kim didn't see any signs it would turn wild.

Isabel Rogers beamed as she surveyed the room full of people. "My job is so much easier when Justin drives well."

A crowd surrounded Justin, hanging on his every word. Kim grinned; it always amused her to see the once grubby-kneed younger cousin whom she'd helped with his math homework—who was she kidding, she'd done the homework for him—the focus of so much attention and adulation.

"You make it look easy no matter how he drives," Kim said. Isabel handled most of the team's hostess duties—Fulcrum Racing's reputation for some of the best parties in NASCAR was entirely to her credit.

Isabel smiled her thanks, but concern shadowed her brown eyes. "The only person who's putting a damper on things is Hugo. Look how gloomy he is tonight."

Following her friend's gaze, Kim found her father across the other side of the room, talking to a couple of sponsor executives. He wasn't grinning from ear to ear, but Kim wouldn't have said he looked unhappy. Still, Isabel had excellent instincts where he was concerned.

"Have you seen much of him this week?" she asked.

Isabel shook her head. "I sometimes wonder if he's losing interest in me." Her tone stayed light, but she bit her lip.

"How could any man lose interest in you?" Kim eyed her friend's deep red dress with the thin straps that flattered her still-smooth shoulders. Isabel stood a couple of inches shorter than Kim's five-eight, but high heels made up for that, and her natural elegance and curvy figure drew people's attention. And Isabel's beauty went way beyond the surface. Kim would love for her dad to marry a wonderful, warm woman like her.

She wanted to see him truly happy, wanted to hear the enormous, booming laugh that was one of her earliest memories, but which had disappeared with Sylvie. It was ironic, she thought, that while she was trying to get a life, her father might throw away his own chance for happiness. Maybe Kim should give him a hurry-up...but no one hurried Hugo.

Isabel snagged a glass of sparkling water from a tray carried by a passing waiter. She said with forced brightness, "Whatever is bothering him, it's not your health. He told me your doctor's happy with the way things are going?"

"Uh, yeah." Kim's lie by omission to her father suddenly became an active falsehood. She hurried to change the subject. "Look, Wade's talking to Dad. We'd better go over there in case they argue in front of the sponsor."

She didn't for a moment think her father would do that, but she knew the suggestion would override Isabel's hesitation in approaching Hugo. Maybe all her dad needed was for Isabel to give him a little more encouragement. Her friend used her chatty style to hide the emotional reserve beneath. Maybe Hugo just didn't realize how much she cared.

At the thought of Fulcrum Racing's reputation at stake, Isabel headed toward the knot of men. Kim had to trot to keep up.

A fond smile warmed Hugo's face when he saw Kim. Then, to her shock, his expression blanked when he registered Isabel's presence.

"Hi, Dad," Kim said cheerfully, to cover an awkward pause. "Terrific race today." Her smile encompassed Wade and the sponsors, as well as her dad. It was hard not to let her gaze linger on Wade, who looked devastating in his black jeans and dark shirt.

"Terrific," Wade agreed. But Kim would bet money he wasn't talking about the race. His gaze scanned her face, her figure, then reached her toes. He looked... interested.

Don't panic, Kim told her racing pulse. While her mind asked, *What does he want with me?*

STANDING NEXT TO HUGO made Isabel feel as if one day her world would be right again. Men like him—solid, capable, dependable—were the backbone of NASCAR. Small wonder her hopes for Fulcrum Racing and her hopes for Hugo were intertwined.

She put her hand on his arm. It was solid, too. Strong. "You did a wonderful job out there, as always," she said. "When Justin came out of Turn Two just as Kent rear-ended Will Branch I thought he'd never get out of the way."

"Wade suggested an adjustment midrace that made all the difference." Hugo's hard gaze rested on his car chief.

"Good work," Isabel said to Wade, then pressed her lips together so she wouldn't burble about the race.

Hugo had told her once that his ex-wife Sylvie had given him a sense of quiet, of peace within himself. He hadn't said it in direct comparison to Isabel, who was famous for her loquaciousness, but she'd cringed.

She risked edging closer to Hugo so that her arm brushed his. And parted her lips just enough to let out a relieved breath when he didn't pull away.

Hugo went on to make the same point to the sponsors that Isabel would have, about how the last time a Fulcrum Racing driver had won the NASCAR Sprint Cup Series championship, it had all come down to cornering. Anger flared inside her—at Hugo, at herself.

She was sick of worrying that he might not love her, sick of the fear that made her second-guess her words and actions. They'd been dating almost three months—surely she should be confident of his feelings by now? It didn't help that they were still hiding their relationship.

Across the room, Isabel's brother Dixon caught her eye. He jerked his head to summon her. But she wasn't about to leave Hugo's side, not when her arm through his felt like a tenuous reconnection after weeks of distance.

So Dixon came to her.

"Isabel, meet Clay Mortimer." He sounded his urbane self, but his eyes telegraphed bad news as he introduced her to the man beside him. "This is Clay's first time at a NASCAR race."

Clay Mortimer, the new owner of Turn-Rite Tools, wasn't reputed to be a NASCAR fan. So Isabel wholeheartedly supported her brother's goal for the evening: to keep Mortimer happy and make sure Turn-Rite Tools stayed on as sponsor.

She detached herself from Hugo—and tried not to notice that he unconsciously shook his arm, as if to rid himself of all memory of the contact. She forced a smile as she spoke to Clay. "I'm so pleased to meet you."

Clay wasn't overly tall—about the same height as Isabel in her heels—but he was broad-shouldered, solidly built. He'd shaved his head the way middle-aged men did when they'd lost more hair than they liked to admit to. It lent a toughness to his appearance that, in concert with sharp blue eyes and a tiny white scar at one corner of his mouth, suggested he didn't suffer fools gladly. The hand that engulfed Isabel's was predictably strong, the fingers blunt and work-roughened.

He wore a chunky gold signet ring on the little finger of his right hand, and Isabel felt the weight of it against her flesh. Something in its flashy heaviness asserted that Clay Mortimer might be a millionaire many times over, but he'd got there by hard work, not pedigree or privilege.

"My sister is our VP sponsor liaison," Dixon said. "She knows everyone in NASCAR and has her finger on the opportunities that help our sponsors increase the return on their investment."

Isabel exchanged a smile with Dixon—this was what their family had always been about, working in perfect synchronicity for the good of Fulcrum Racing.

"You picked a great place to attend your first race," she said to Clay. "Few tracks offer the variety of Watkins Glen, so we get to see the drivers tested in all kinds of ways. And as a sponsor, you must have been doubly thrilled with Justin's success after such a—"

"I was, until I figured out how much it cost me."

Clay's voice had a roughened edge that grated on Isabel's senses, and not just because he'd interrupted her.

No wonder Dixon looked panicked. He believed the decision to pour millions of dollars into a NASCAR sponsorship was a no-brainer. So did Isabel. Normally, she would relish the chance to exercise her persuasive talents on Clay, but tonight, she struggled to summon the energy.

She found it in the end, managed to laugh in a way that was sympathetic, but conveyed the right amount of disbelief that Clay could really mean what he'd said.

"Why don't you and I get some food?" she said smoothly. "Then I'll tell you more about the team." From the corner of her eye, she saw a dark-haired woman, at least ten years younger than Isabel, chatting to Hugo. She stiffened, then consciously relaxed as her focus returned to Clay.

He was watching her, a small smile curving his mouth. It was probably his best feature, the lips full enough to be sensuous, yet entirely masculine. Isabel told herself the reason his mouth was so noticeable was because he didn't have any hair. She tossed her own hair, which fell in loose waves below her shoulders. "Dinner?" she prompted Clay.

He shrugged and allowed her to lead him to the buffet counter. When they'd heaped their plates with roast beef rolls and salad, they sat at one of the suite's small dining tables.

While Clay ate, Isabel kept up a monologue about the history of Fulcrum Racing, about Justin's driving, about NASCAR racing and the rich rewards it offered its fans. And the very real monetary rewards it offered its sponsors. At one point, she signaled a waiter to replace Clay's empty beer bottle and to replenish her mineral water, but she didn't break her flow.

When she paused to take a sip of her water, Clay tossed a couple of questions at her. They were detailed about fiscal matters and asked with an edge of criticism.

Isabel had every number he could possibly want at her fingertips. She answered his questions, then finished with a flourish. "Research completed in April demonstrated that since Turn-Rite began sponsoring Justin, its brand recognition has improved sixty percent." She sent up a prayer of thanks for her own foresight in persuading Turn-Rite's previous owner to commission the survey.

"I understand we also upped our TV advertising early this year," Clay said. "It's anyone's guess as to which expenditure was responsible for the increase in recognition."

"Probably a combination of the two," she admitted. "You're making multiple impressions on the consumer, so that when they go to the hardware store, they choose Turn-Rite."

He fired off several more questions, all requiring her to think hard. The conversation was exhausting, perhaps because she'd started it emotionally drained. The rest of the room faded from Isabel's consciousness; all that mattered was getting her points across to Clay.

She gave it her best shot, stopping only when she'd furnished him with every possible angle on a NASCAR sponsorship to mull over.

"What do you think?" She looked expectantly at Clay, who by now had emptied his plate.

"I think," he said slowly, "I've never heard anyone talk for so long without taking a breath as you just did."

What? She'd poured her heart and soul into telling him exactly how Fulcrum Racing was good for his business, and he thought she *talked* too much?

The elastic band of Isabel's emotions, stretched tighter and tighter over the last few weeks, finally snapped, propelling her out of her seat so fast she jolted the table. Clay's beer bottle toppled over.

"You—" Several insults sprang to mind, of which *jerk* was the mildest. She swallowed them all and kept her tone low but intense. "You asked me a number of questions. I answered them."

Without looking down, she righted the beer bottle. Ignoring the dampness still spreading over the dark orange cloth, she planted her hands on the table and leaned in toward Clay. It put her disturbingly close to that sensuous mouth, but she refused to back off.

"If you wanted me to answer in fifty words or less, you should have said so. Because I can do that—Turn-Rite Tools is one of an elite group of companies sponsoring the best racing in the world. Thanks to its links with Fulcrum Racing, consumers associate the Turn-Rite brand with quality and performance. Your NASCAR sponsorship would be cheap at twice the price."

She had no idea how many words that was, and that last sentence was brazen exaggeration. Isabel was suddenly aware that her cheeks were hot, that she was breathing heavily and that Clay was eyeing her with interest.

"Nice job, Isabel," he said. "You're very passionate about your work, and I like passionate people."

Isabel's first reaction was relief that he hadn't taken her outburst as rudeness. Then something crackled between them, a current of awareness. Clay's blue eyes held hers until she dragged them away. She concentrated on spreading her napkin over the dark stain on the tablecloth. As if covering up the problem would set everything right.

"We're all passionate here at Fulcrum Racing," she said, trying to quell that odd awareness with her matter-of-fact tone, "so we should work well together."

Clay didn't say anything, just watched her hands as she smoothed out the napkin.

"Another beer?" she asked, mindful he'd only half finished the last one before she knocked it over.

He shook his head, rubbed his stomach to suggest he'd had all the food and drink he could handle. He drummed his fingers on the table. By the time he spoke, Isabel's nerves were ready to shatter.

"Like I said, you did a nice job just now." He crumpled his napkin, tossed it onto the table. "I appreciate plain speaking, so I'm going to tell you straight where I'm coming from."

Although that explained why she hadn't offended him just now, Isabel was not generally a fan of plain speaking. She valued the social niceties that smoothed the conversational path.

Clay said, "I paid a lot of money for Turn-Rite Tools because its gross profits are exceptional. But the company's costs are too high. I plan to fix that." He leaned back in his seat. "We spend too much on marketing, and the biggest item in the budget is NASCAR. As of now, it's under review."

She'd known she might have to prepare a new business case for Turn-Rite to justify its ongoing investment, and was a hundred percent confident she could make her case…yet, still, she caught her breath. "I hope you'll give the decision very careful consideration," she said.

"I'll crunch the numbers with due care and attention." But his tone suggested he would dismiss them.

"Numbers are important," Isabel said, "but you need to weigh the intangibles, too."

Clay's shaved head, the bulk of his shoulders, his big hands, suggested he would steamroller over anything less tangible than a semitrailer without registering the bump. "You're at a NASCAR race for the first time," she said, "and although I'm sure you're a quick study, there's a lot more to this sport than you realize."

"Whatever I need to know, I daresay you'll tell me."

She would…but she sensed the obvious methods—the heavyweight business case backed up by some serious schmoozing—might not convince him.

"Good night, Isabel," he said, and stood to leave.

Isabel had to fight the instinct to hold on to him, to say some more.

Because failure wasn't an option. If Turn-Rite Tools pulled out, the urgent need to find another sponsor for Justin would derail Fulcrum Racing's plans to run a third car next season. The third car they'd announced so boldly to the press. The average fan might not care, but to NASCAR insiders it would signify that Fulcrum Racing was more hot air than substance, that the Rogerses had lost their footing as one of NASCAR's leading families once and for all.

"SO IF A GUY TAKES you to dinner," Wade said, his lazy smile traveling over Kim's blue silk dress and down her legs, "do you give him a list of conversation topics to study first? So your powerful intellect doesn't get bored?"

Just about every question he'd asked had been a variation on how a guy got a date with Kim.

"The guys I date already know a lot about the things that interest me," she said, ignoring that garbage about her powerful intellect.

"Uh-huh." He took a swig of his beer. "NASCAR interests you, right?"

Kim giggled, a breathy sound that, to her alarm, was reminiscent of the redhead who'd approached him in the garage yesterday. But that woman probably had a life, and Kim didn't, so maybe she shouldn't worry.

While they'd been talking, she'd figured out the answer to the question of why Wade wanted to date her— she didn't believe mysteries should stay unexplained.

This one was simple. Having resolved to get a life, which at the most basic biological level meant connecting with one's species to ensure procreation, she was now sending out unconscious, subliminal signals that Wade—a man in touch, she suspected, with his elemental nature—was picking up.

"Great, let's go." He put his beer bottle down on the bar.

"No way." No matter how enticing the prospect of crossing a jock-date off her list, dinner with Wade was well past her personal fear boundary.

CHAPTER FIVE

"HEY, YOU TWO." ISABEL approached, her cheeks flushed and her eyes bright. Although the bartender was clearing up, she asked him for a glass of white wine. When it arrived, she slugged two large gulps.

"Hard night?" Kim asked. She figured Isabel had to be smarting from Hugo's lack of response earlier.

"You have no idea." Isabel took another long slug, then reluctantly handed the glass back to the bartender. She gripped the edge of the bar and closed her eyes for a couple of seconds, as if she was waiting for the alcohol to take effect.

Kim and Wade watched her in curious silence. Not for long. Unlike Kim, Isabel considered silence to be a social disaster on the scale of flossing at the dinner table, so her eyes soon snapped open. Crossly, she said, "Could you two talk, please? About something pleasant, something simple?"

"About me." Justin joined them, having at last finished schmoozing with every person in the room who wanted a piece of a NASCAR driver. "I'm simple."

"You're selling yourself short," Wade said, and Isabel visibly relaxed as the conversational ball was taken from her hands. "You did a damn good job of turning right today, too."

"I'm versatile," Justin said modestly. "Just as long as I don't have to go both directions at once."

Rachel and her fiancé, Payton, swelled their group. Rachel slipped her arm through Justin's. "You may be talented, little brother—" she was all of one year older than he was "—but without those crash-hot engines I build for you every week, you'd be toast."

"You did a great job with the engine today," Wade told her seriously.

Rachel raised her eyebrows. "Er, thanks, Wade."

Maybe Rachel was wrong, and Wade wasn't after the crew chief job, Kim thought. She took advantage of Justin's and Rachel's ensuing banter to speak to Isabel. "I'm certain Dad didn't snub you deliberately. He's just preoccupied."

Isabel slid a glance at Wade, who didn't look as if he was listening, but nor was he joining in with the others. She lowered her voice. "He hasn't said more than two words to me all night." She twisted her fingers, an uncharacteristically nervous gesture. "I really need to get some time alone with him." She turned away to say goodbye to Justin, who was leaving now that he'd spent the two hours at the party specified in his contract. As soon as he departed, most of the remaining guests did, too.

Hugo came over. "Kim, if you're ready, I'll drop you at your hotel."

Before she could agree, Wade spoke up. "Actually, Hugo, Kim's coming to dinner with me. But Isabel needs a ride."

With Isabel shining with gratitude toward Wade at the thought of getting Hugo alone, Kim couldn't contradict him. The jock had been listening in to their conversation after all.

She directed a tight smile at Wade. "I'm pretty tired, I don't want to be out late."

"We'll eat fast," he promised, magnanimous in victory, "even if I have to get indigestion."

With her eyes she conveyed her fervent hope that would be the outcome. He grinned, and shepherded her toward the door.

He'd outmaneuvered her, and he was enjoying it. *Everyone gets a lucky break sometimes.* Challenge zinged through Kim's veins, the kind of challenge she normally got from starting a groundbreaking research project.

Wade wouldn't win again.

WADE DROVE TO A lakefront restaurant just outside the village of Watkins Glen. It was dark—nearly nine o'clock—when they pulled into the parking lot, which meant they couldn't see the water. But Kim heard the splash of a night creature on the lake, and the breeze-blown lapping of water against a jetty.

Inside the rustic-style building, they were shown to a table tucked discreetly into a corner. Romantic.

A waiter brought a bread basket, and Kim dug into it. She lacked the capacity to eat and make small talk with strangers at the same time, so she'd held back from the buffet at the party. She was starving.

"Mmm." She savored a mouthful of the warm, crusty bread. "This almost makes me forgive you for listening in to my private conversation with Isabel."

"Yeah, that was quite illuminating—I had no idea she and Hugo were dating." Wade buttered his bread roll.

"I'm very driven when I want something. Probably best you learn that now."

Arrogant jock! He'd coerced her into one date and thought she was his to command. "Thanks, but I try not to store extraneous information," she said. "It interferes with the processing of the important stuff."

He grinned, and raised his water glass to her in salute.

They ordered their entrées—steak for Kim, since it was important to keep her protein and iron levels up. Besides, she didn't want to put on her nerdy glasses to read the menu, so steak was an easy option. Wade chose pasta with a robust sauce of tomatoes, green peppers and pepperoni.

Kim sat back, spread her fingers on the tablecloth and relaxed the muscles that had been tensed throughout the party. She hadn't intended to come out with Wade, but now that she was here, she might as well enjoy the experience for the first and last time.

When he offered her a drink, she shunned the diet soda she'd been drinking earlier and ordered a glass of Chianti. He ordered a beer. Then Wade said, "The word around the workshop is that you're sick. Something to do with your kidneys."

She'd hoped he hadn't heard about that. And yet…if he had, and he'd still asked her out for dinner, surely it said good things about his character?

Kim finished her mouthful of bread. "I was diagnosed with kidney disease a few months ago. I've been on dialysis since then, and it's working well." Or at least, it *was*.

"Dialysis sounds serious." Wade looked as if he was worried she might whip out a bag of dialysate fluid and start right there at the table. Which she almost wished she could—she was tired, and she wouldn't be back at her hotel in time to start her ten o'clock session. It didn't matter too much if she was late occasionally, but she always liked to allow time for contingencies.

"It's no big deal," she said. "And it's only until I get my transplant."

Wade recoiled. "You need a transplant?"

Kim could see their date going downhill from here as she grossed him out. "It's a straightforward procedure these days—it's just a matter of waiting for a donor."

She didn't add that seventy thousand Americans were currently waiting for a kidney transplant, and nearly all of them had a better chance of getting one than Kim. "So," she said, "how did you end up at Fulcrum Racing?"

WADE GAVE KIM A potted history of his motor sports career, but all the time he was planning how to bring the conversation back to her medical condition, so he could get the answers Hugo wanted. Did Hugo know she needed a transplant?

As he talked, he watched her across the table, the smooth fall of her hair to her shoulders, her fine, expressive features. She looked…touchable.

Wade dragged his mind back to the conclusion of his story. "And then your dad hired me as Justin's car chief," he said.

"I hear you and Dad don't get along," she said when he reached the end of his account. She added hastily, "He's never said that."

Isabel Rogers had, Wade assumed. Kim and Isabel had seemed pretty chummy.

"Hugo and I have different styles," he agreed. A hell of an understatement.

She cocked her head to one side. "When people talk about Dad, they use words like considered, knowledgeable, strong."

"In other words, cautious, fact-bound, stubborn," Wade said.

Kim's forehead creased. Then she smiled—the first unguarded smile he'd seen from her. It transformed her face, lit her from within.

"I guess Dad can be all of those things," she said with fond resignation. She leaned back while the waiter set her entrée in front of her. "Mmm, this smells great. So, how do people describe you?"

Wade took a moment to inhale the spicy aroma of his own meal. "They might say instinctive…focused… tough."

She picked up her knife and fork as she considered him. "In other words, impulsive, insensitive to others' opinions, difficult."

For a startled moment, he thought Hugo had discussed him with her. But all she'd done was flip the coins of his self-assessment, as he'd done about Hugo. Smart lady. But then, he knew that.

"Touché," he said dryly.

She was too smart to let him push her somewhere she didn't want to go in a conversation. If he was to have any chance of finding out the truth about her health, he needed to build her trust. He quashed the thought that he would be building her trust purely so he could breach it by tattling to her father.

Now that he knew she needed a transplant, he had

more sympathy for Hugo's request. No matter how much the truth hurt, Wade would have been furious if his father had kept the extent of his illness from the family.

The way to build trust was to be open. So when Kim said, "Are your folks NASCAR fans?" he prepared to spill enough beans to encourage her to reciprocate.

"Mom enjoys the occasional race, but all my siblings love it."

"*All* your siblings?" Her fork paused halfway to her mouth. "How many?"

"I'm the oldest of seven," he said. "Number five was another boy, the rest are girls."

"Your parents must be exhausted."

He smiled faintly. "Mom's in pretty good shape. My dad died when I was seventeen."

"Wade, I'm sorry." She reached across the table, touched his hand. Her fingers were light, smooth, warming.

"He had Lou Gehrig's disease—you know it?"

"I understand it's a wasting condition," she said. "One that can progress very slowly."

"Dad was sick for two years, which isn't bad," Wade said crisply. "But he'd been a pretty active guy all his life. By the time he went, he'd had enough."

She looked sad on his behalf, and he wanted to touch a finger to her lips, tilt them upward.

"I suppose your family had time to prepare emotionally," she said. "Did that help?"

He shrugged. "I don't know. My folks are…volatile." He realized that was one thing he liked about Kim. Once she'd gotten over her stuttering, she'd turned out to be pretty calm. He would have said restful, but that megabrain of hers was always so busy, he had to be constantly ready to stand his ground, to fight back when necessary.

"My great-great-grandparents on my father's side came to the U.S.A. from Lebanon," he said. "They left behind a lot of old customs, but not the tendency to overreact. My mom is of Italian stock, and her family has the same problem. My sisters can scream louder than a track full of race cars over a new pair of shoes."

Kim laughed, and there was a wistful quality to it. She'd read, correctly, that Wade thought the world of his sisters, and they thought the same of him. "I guess you became the man of the family when your dad died," she said.

"Uh-huh." Long before that, Wade thought. From the moment of his dad's diagnosis, the whole family had plunged into a two-year grief-fest. With six women in the family, including his mom, it seemed as if every time Wade turned around, someone was crying. Life had been put on hold.

His father had been like Wade—more logical, practical. "This is their way of coping," he'd told Wade. "They need to let it out."

"Do they need to let it out so loudly and so often?" Wade, just turned sixteen, had demanded in frustration. His younger brother had been ten years old, and also prone to tears. Some days, Wade and his dad had the only dry eyes in the house.

"Hey, at least I know they care," Dad had joked, the words slurred by his illness.

"I care," Wade had said fiercely, shocked that his lack of public emotion might give the wrong impression.

"Son—" his father had grabbed his hand in a grip that

was stronger than he'd had in a while "—I know you do. I worry that you care too much. You take on board everyone else's problems. When I'm gone, your mom and your sisters will look to you for leadership, and I know you're the man to give it. But if you let every little thing get to you, you'll never survive."

"You're saying I shouldn't care?" Wade had said, confused.

"I'm saying, keep a part of yourself back, for your own sanity." His father had released his grip and closed his eyes for a second. "Make sure you don't have your guts ripped out every time you have to make a decision."

It had been good advice—it had taken only a couple of months for Wade to realize that. He couldn't always detach from the emotions—he'd been too young—but when he did, he made smarter decisions. What's more, his sisters and his mother argued less about them.

"You're like me," Kim said thoughtfully. "You probably didn't get to do a lot of the things your friends did."

"I drank my share of beer, had my share of dates." But he nearly always got home sober enough to make sure he didn't have a hangover.

She speared a piece of steak with her fork, added a French fry. "Did you get to college?"

He shook his head. "Dad's life insurance covered the basics, and Mom did some sewing from home. But she had her hands full with the younger kids and we needed a steady wage coming in. I got a job as an apprentice mechanic with a team in the NASCAR Whelen All-American Series. I worked my way up to crew chief, then switched to NASCAR's national series."

While his siblings were still in school it had been an

awkward juggling act—working to the high standard he set himself, getting promoted as often as possible, but still leaving time for family when they needed him. For a few high-pressure years, he'd only taken jobs based in the workshop—he hadn't been part of the team that traveled to the races each week.

"But now," he said, "the kids have all grown up. Sarah, my baby sister, just finished her nursing degree. Mom's still young and healthy. Now, I get to go after what I want."

This moment had been forever coming, which was why he was so determined to achieve his goal. Because although he'd had the reward of seeing his family come out of those years intact—stronger than ever, in fact—it had taken something out of him. Left him empty inside. Focusing on his dream of becoming a crew chief would fill him up again.

Kim took a mouthful of steak and chewed it thoughtfully. The way she did everything. "So what exactly do you want?"

It wasn't a secret. "I want to be the crew chief for Fulcrum Racing's new car."

Her eyes widened. "But I thought—" She stopped.

Wade finished his beer, set the bottle down. "You thought Rachel was lined up for the job?"

She nodded. "That was nice of you to tell Rachel she did a good job on the engine tonight, given you're both after the crew chief role."

He shrugged. "She deserved it. That was some engine."

She put down her cutlery, dabbed at her mouth with a napkin. "Is that why you asked me to dinner?"

"What do you mean?" He shifted in his seat.

"Did you ask me out because you want me to put in a good word for you with Dad?" Her clear gray eyes were curious, not accusing.

"No," he said, relieved he could answer honestly.

"Because I won't," she said. "Rachel's family, I won't go against her."

"I don't expect you to."

"So," she said, "why *did* you ask me out?"

"*You* asked *me*."

She frowned, and two little lines appeared in the middle of her forehead. "I let you off the hook, but you insisted. I can't think why."

"I like you," he said, and realized he meant it, even if that wasn't why he'd pursued the dinner date.

Her frown deepened, and she pushed her hair back behind her ears. "Really?"

"What's not to like?" He pushed his plate away. "You have a great figure—"

"I've put on seven pounds in the last two months."

"Then you were too skinny before." He continued as if she hadn't interrupted, "You make me laugh, you're smart—though you're scared to move out of your comfort zone."

"I'm not scared."

"You're a 'fraidy-cat," he said firmly. "But I like you."

Just when it seemed she would protest some more, Kim pressed her lips together. Wade folded his arms across his chest. "You're pretty," he said. "The color of your hair reminds me of baklava."

HIS MENTION OF THE honey-filled Middle Eastern pastry dessert jolted Kim. She'd never been paid a compliment made especially for her before and it left her feeling strangely weak. She fingered a lock of her hair— it was safer than meeting Wade's gaze.

He was a practiced flirt, according to Rachel. Maybe he talked this way to every women he dated.

"What about your taste in men?" he said. "I assume you don't have a boyfriend, given that you asked me to dinner?"

"I broke up with someone a month ago, but it wasn't serious."

"Was the breakup because of your health?"

"No," she said, annoyed. "I can date, just like anyone else. The relationship ran its course."

"Why did you ask me out?" he said. "You didn't really have the hots for me, did you?"

"You're very attractive," she said fairly, then paused. "It was a spur-of-the-moment thing."

"You don't do spur of the moment."

How had he figured that out?

"The old me doesn't do spur of the moment," she said. "The new me—"

"Why do you need a new you?" he interrupted. "What was wrong with the old one?"

"The old one's life was too tame," she said. "I wanted to do something…adventurous. Then I saw you." She spread her hands as if the rest was obvious.

"Asking a guy to have coffee is your idea of adventurous?" He shook his head, disbelieving. "Did you think about skydiving?"

"It's all relative."

He was looking at her as if she had the courage of a bowl of jelly. In self-defense, suddenly anxious that he shouldn't think her pathetic, Kim reached into her purse and pulled out the folded list that she now carried everywhere, like a talisman against her boring life.

She waved it at him. "If I'd been starting from scratch I'm sure I'd have planned something more challenging. But I came across a list I wrote back in college and that triggered my decision."

Wade rubbed his chin. "What kind of list?"

She nibbled on her lower lip. Could she tell him? "You have to know where I was coming from when I wrote it. I fast-tracked through high school and college, so I never got to do a lot of the things other girls did."

"You mean—" he leaned forward, interested now "—things like make out at the movies?"

Kim gaped, shielded the list with her hand as if it had suddenly turned transparent. "How did you know?"

He laughed, and the deep, attractive sound turned heads at nearby tables. "*Everyone* made out at the movies."

"I didn't," she said crossly. "And could you keep your voice down? The whole restaurant doesn't need to know I'm a loser."

His look was speculative, but he said more quietly, "What else didn't you do?"

She gripped the list tighter. "I'm not telling."

It soon became obvious who was the big, strong NASCAR car chief around here and who was the puny scientist. In one swift movement he snatched the list from her.

"Give that back." She tried to grab it, but her arms were shorter than his.

Wade began reading. Almost immediately, his lips twitched, and he darted a quick glance at Kim. Somewhere lower than her face. *The push-up bra.* Hastily, she folded her arms across her chest, and his smile widened.

"You've seen the list," she said. "Now I'd like it back."

He held it farther out of her reach. "Are you allowed to get a tattoo when you're on dialysis?"

"My doctor says it's fine, as long as I choose a reputable studio and keep an eye out for infection afterward."

Wade read down the list with a frown that deepened. And deepened. Kim braced herself.

She knew when he got there. His head shot up, accusation burned in his dark eyes. "You asked me to dinner because you want to date a jock?"

CHAPTER SIX

WHATEVER WADE HAD EXPECTED to find on her list, it wasn't that Kim had asked him out because he was Rent-a-Jock! But the evidence was right in front of him, on this scrap of paper and in Kim's transparent-as-hell guilty face.

"I was *seventeen* when I wrote that," she said, a distinction Wade considered irrelevant. She was here on a date with him: enough said. He shook his head, still trying to get a handle on this.

"I'm sorry," Kim said. "You've just been saying those nice things about me...well, maybe they were about me," she babbled in a sudden endearing surge of insecurity. "Or maybe you know a whole bunch of women with baklava-colored hair. But still, you said them, and...well, all along I've been using you."

Wade put a hand to his heart. He said slowly, heavily, "I feel so...so cheap, so sullied."

Kim blinked rapidly; Wade thought he saw the shimmer of tears on her lashes. "No, you mustn't," she said. "Please, I'm sorry, I didn't mean—"

He couldn't hold out another second. He burst out laughing. Kim stared. Then her lips tightened. "Oh, you..." She balled up her napkin and threw it at him. It fell short, landing in the remains of his pasta. Still laughing, Wade fished it out.

"I can't believe your irresistible attraction to me was phony." He flicked the list. "What else is on here?"

He read down the page, found *Make out at the movies,* the inspired guess of his that had unnerved her. And below it, *Dump the jock.* He raised an eyebrow, shot her a querying glance. "When can I expect to be dumped?"

"You'll be the first to know," she promised.

He smiled, then glanced back at the piece of card. "Why is *Find Mom* crossed out?"

She stiffened. "That was important when I was a teenager. It's been so long since I've seen my mother, it no longer matters."

Wade tried to remember what he'd heard about Hugo's ex-wife. Only that they'd split up a long time ago. "You don't know where she is?"

"She left when I was four. Dad and I haven't heard from her since." Kim's tone was neutral, and for once he couldn't read her face, which told him just how painful the subject was.

"I'm sorry," he said, and handed the list back.

Kim stuffed it into her purse.

But he wasn't done with his questions. He speared her with his gaze. "The list says *Before I die.*"

Just saying the words sent lead through his veins, making his limbs heavy.

"I was a kid," she said patiently. "At the time, it seemed tragic that I hadn't done this stuff. That heading has nothing to do with my underperforming kidneys. Apart from tiring easily, I'm fine."

Was this the answer he'd been hanging out for all

night? Her gray eyes were clear, honest, intelligent. Wade knew firsthand how people reacted to serious illness, and it wasn't with the calm certainty Kim displayed. He figured she had to be telling the truth.

Everything lightened up again, as relief surged through him, a wave of energy peculiar in its intensity. Maybe that was because now he could report back to her father without betraying a confidence. And her crazy list had freed him from any sense of guilt—her motives for dating him were every bit as impure as his.

"What happens now?" he asked. "You're planning on doing the things on this list?"

Kim leaned back while the waiter delivered their coffees. "I already played hooky."

He laughed at the pride in her voice. "What's next?"

She blinked, then fidgeted with the strap of her purse. "I'm still in the planning phase."

"You wrote the list, what, fifteen years ago?"

She nodded.

"That sounds like plenty of time for planning," he said. "You need to get started. No more procrastination."

She bristled, and he figured she didn't like being told what to do any more than he did. Her eyes sparked, and she said admiringly, "My, what a big word."

"I learned it from a cereal packet." But Wade wasn't about to let her distract him, no matter how much he enjoyed her humor. "If you prefer single syllables, seize the day."

Her eyes widened. She looked as if she might say something, then changed her mind. "I appreciate your interest," she said stiffly. "But I'll do this my way."

They finished their coffees in near silence, and Wade

asked for the check. Kim pulled out her wallet, but he fixed her with a frown that had her tucking it away again. A smart woman like her should have figured out that going Dutch wouldn't be a jock's style.

KIM EASED BACK INTO her seat in Wade's classic Mustang, suddenly exhausted. He helped her clip her seat belt, then headed for the hotel where they were both staying.

Kim's body might be tired, but her mind raced the entire journey. Into unfamiliar, possibly dangerous territory. Did eating dinner with Wade count as a date, or should she kiss him, just to be sure? She was shocked at how easily she could picture his firm, well-molded lips, without so much as a sidelong glance at him. And some people considered sex to be an automatic part of a date these days. Not her, of course. But did Wade? Her face burned at the thought. And she discovered that putting Wade and sexual intimacy in the same mind space kindled another burning, deep inside her.

Too soon, they arrived. Wade escorted Kim to her room, and used her cardkey to open the door.

"Uh, thanks," she said, "I had a nice evening."

He took her hands loosely in his.

"You realize I have to kiss you good-night," he said, simultaneously relieving her by bringing the question out into the open and alarming her.

She took a step backward. "You think?"

"I'm very familiar with the date-a-jock scenario. Trust me, this is how it works."

WADE FIGURED THAT, given a choice, Kim would want another fifteen years to plan a good-night kiss. Too bad.

He'd told her he was going to kiss her, which he considered mighty considerate and more than enough warning, and now it was time to act. He pulled her into his arms—she fit so snugly, it was both foreign and intensely familiar.

Her fingers curled around his upper arms, and the heat of her touch manacled him. He couldn't have moved away if he tried.

"Wade, I don't think—"

"Great idea," he said huskily. "Don't think, Little Ms. Brain Box."

He followed his own advice, putting aside all thought of how this might not be a smart thing to do as he joined his mouth to hers. That very first contact seared through him and he wanted to force her lips apart, explore every nuance of her mouth. But he didn't. If she really hadn't done even half the stuff on that list of hers, she'd probably freak out.

He kept the kiss gentle, but firm, and enjoyed the contour of her mouth, its slight quiver beneath his. His tongue traced the fullness of her lower lip, then slipped inside, but not too far. Mmm, she tasted sweet, honeyed, like that baklava he'd mentioned earlier. Wade's senses stirred—who would have thought such a tame kiss could be so enjoyable? Kim made a little sound that he read as pleasure, and immediately the need to take it further consumed him. He couldn't, not without losing some of his mammoth self-control, a revelation that surprised him. So he stopped. Reluctantly.

But he continued to hold her in his arms, his chin resting on the top of her head. "Mmm," he said.

"Hmm," she said, a sound that held more curiosity than satisfaction.

Wade drew away so he could see her face. She looked pensive. "What?"

She shook her head. "Nothing."

As if Kim Murphy ever thought *nothing*. "Tell me," he said, looking forward to hearing whatever she'd come up with now.

"I guess I thought…I expected…" Her cheeks turned pink. "Really, it's nothing."

"What?" he demanded.

"I…well, *logic* suggests," she said delicately, "that a jock would have a, uh, superior kissing technique to other men. Maybe because he gets more practice, or maybe because he's naturally better at it."

"Just because I've kissed a lot of women," he said, wanting to reassure her, "that doesn't mean what you and I did wasn't special."

She winced and said apologetically, "The thing is, that kiss that you and I just…kissed…wasn't as exciting as logic dictated."

What the— This was what he got for trying to be a gentleman?

"It's nothing personal," she said.

Wade considered hauling her back into his arms and taking her mouth in a crushing kiss that would prove to both their satisfaction that the chemistry between them was at the combustible end of the scale. But that would show her that he had indeed taken her comment very personally. No doubt she'd once again brand him as Neanderthal.

"Next time I kiss you—" he only just managed to

keep a caveman growl out of the words "—will be very different."

Kim's gaze rested on his lips, then slid.

"Next time I kiss you," he said again, slowly and clearly, "prepare for it to blow your mind."

She blinked rapidly, and edged back into her room, positioning herself behind the door as if she were about to close it. She wrapped her fingers around the edge of the door.

"Good night, 'fraidy-cat," Wade said.

Safely beyond reach, she said, "I'm not afraid of a kiss."

He reached out, brushed a knuckle against her cheek. "Maybe you should be." He sauntered down the corridor, and grinned when he heard her door slam.

WADE'S CELL PHONE RANG just as he set it on the night-stand in his hotel room. Hugo.

"Any news?" his boss asked.

I kissed your daughter and she told me I tanked.

Wade sat on the bed. "Kim said she's fine, just a bit tired."

Hugo tutted. "Did you believe her?"

"I'm not sure." Wade ran a hand over his face. He'd thought she was completely transparent, until she'd closed up when she spoke about her mother. What else had she hidden from him?

"Wade?" Hugo said sharply, reminding him he'd let the silence run on.

Should he tell Hugo, or shouldn't he? He had to. "Did you know Kim needs a transplant?" *Sorry, Kim.*

Silence. Then he said, "Of course I did."

Hugo's dismissive tone riled Wade. "Why the heck didn't you tell me?"

"Kim forbade me to share details of her condition with people on the team," Hugo said.

"Dammit, Hugo, if I'd known her condition was that serious…" What? He wouldn't have asked her to dinner? Hell, no. He'd had his fill of medical emergencies, done his share of putting aside his own priorities for the sake of a sick person.

"I asked you to take her to dinner, not marry her," Hugo snapped, obviously reading the direction of Wade's thoughts.

He was right, of course. But Wade had had a damned good night with Kim, and now he felt as if it had been under false pretenses. *It was. She didn't know her dad had asked me to take her out.*

Okay, so maybe he wasn't lily-white in this. "What else haven't you told me?" Wade demanded.

"Nothing," Hugo said. "And the fact that Kim needs a transplant…I guess that sounds a big deal when you're new to the situation. But it's a waiting game, that's all. Some people stay on dialysis twenty years or more before they get a transplant, and they're fine."

Wade knuckled the back of his neck, suddenly tired. He wondered if Kim was in bed yet. "So she doesn't need the transplant urgently?"

"No. Why, did she say she did?" Hugo's voice sharpened.

"Uh-uh."

"The dialysis gives her a normal life," Hugo said. "But I'd like her to have the transplant soon if she can. Did she tell you anything about her mother?"

"Only that she left and Kim hasn't seen her since."

Hugo sighed. "If we can find a live donor match, then we're not dependent on Kim waiting until she gets to the top of the transplant list. I'm trying to find her mom in the hope she'll be a match, or that any other kids she's had might be. But I'm not having much luck."

"When you say you're trying…"

"I can't find any public record of Sylvie's whereabouts, so I've been putting advertisements in personal columns around the country."

It sounded like a hit-and-miss strategy to Wade—good thing Kim's transplant wasn't an emergency.

"I take it you're not a match," he said.

After a second Hugo said, "Kim's my adopted daughter. Her birth father is dead."

Wade's picture of Kim Murphy rearranged itself once again. She was full of surprises. Presumably, losing her mother had been even harder on her, if Hugo wasn't her real father.

"I took the test, of course, but I'm not a match," Hugo said. "The best match is likely to be a relative. If Kim's condition changes, she could need surgery in a hurry, hence my advertisements."

Wade thought back over the evening. "She didn't seem as if she was under that kind of pressure." Kim's preoccupation with trivial things like playing hooky and buying bras—Wade grinned—suggested quite the opposite.

"Will you see her again?" Hugo asked.

"Maybe one more date," Wade said. Because there was that small matter of a mind-blowing kiss that he owed her. "Kim's good company."

"She is," Hugo agreed. Suspicion colored his next words. "You're not seriously interested in her, are you?"

"I like her," Wade said. "But I have enough responsibility in my life that I wouldn't want a relationship with someone who's sick." It was brutally honest, but there was no point pretending. "And Kim made it plain she's not interested in me beyond a couple of dates."

He assumed Hugo had no idea about her list. Wade wasn't about to tell him—just the heading would be enough to have her father worried.

"In that case, I'd appreciate you sharing anything else you find out," Hugo said heavily. And now he didn't sound like the indomitable Hugo Murphy. He sounded like a father who was worried about his daughter, who was frustrated that he didn't have a chance to do what came naturally—protect her.

"I doubt she'll say any more," Wade said, "but if she does, I'll let you know."

Hugo passed a couple of comments about today's race, and Wade responded. When he ended the call, he realized he and his boss had talked for twenty minutes without arguing. That had to be progress. He just had to figure out how to cement that into a solid basis for a promotion.

KIM HAD DATED A jock, she'd kissed him, and it had been…nice enough. But it hadn't been the earth-shattering experience she'd anticipated.

"He probably has so many women throwing themselves at him, he's never had to learn to kiss decently," she grumbled to herself as she walked through the tunnel under the track to the infield at Michigan. Whereas the men Kim dated—scientists, academics—

were smart enough to know that when they were out of their element, they needed to make a big effort.

Not that it necessarily paid off.

And it didn't matter that Wade's kiss had been a disappointment, because she'd dated a jock and now she could move on with her list. In fact, she'd already done that.

Kim flashed her hard card to gain admittance to the garage area. The teams were going through the inspection process, NASCAR officials checking that every car complied with a multitude of regulations.

Everywhere she looked, there were good-looking guys in team uniforms. Some of them had a swagger to their movements that said they knew women were watching them, would be willing to date them later to bask in the reflected glory of a NASCAR team.

"Lousy kissers." Kim applied probability theory, extrapolating out from Wade's kiss to encompass the entire spectrum of NASCAR jocks. Then she realized that one of those lousy kissers was looking directly at her. No, two of them were. And they weren't looking at her face.

The fact that she'd completed number two on her list was apparently noticeable to every man in the place. Kim clenched her hands at her sides so she wouldn't give in to the temptation to cross her arms over her bosom—her newly rounded, full bosom, thanks to her new push-up bra.

Kim had slipped out of her office at lunchtime on Wednesday to make her purchase. She'd bought a new T-shirt as well, a size smaller than usual, because otherwise the bra had no visible effect. Now, she wished she'd stuck with her usual size. As she walked through the garage, it seemed everywhere she looked some man had his eyes on her cleavage.

She tried to focus on the scientific aspects of their scrutiny. It was fascinating, really, how an apparent increase in chest measurement had an exponential effect on her visibility to the opposite sex. Biologists, or maybe sociologists, would doubtlessly have done studies—there must be implications for the future of the species.

I'm not a woman flaunting her curves in a push-up bra, I'm a living, breathing science experiment. She thrust out her chest, and headed toward the Fulcrum Racing garage. *And I'm not afraid of Wade Abraham and his mind-blowing kiss.*

WADE SENSED KIM'S APPROACH, rather than saw her. He continued checking the shock absorbers on the No. 448 car—she wasn't going to distract him from putting the best possible race car out on the track today. No matter how much she'd occupied his mind since their dinner at Watkins Glen.

He held out for a full minute, then couldn't resist sneaking a glance her way. A couple of the guys were talking to her—Mike, the jackman, and Davey, one of the mechanics. There was an edge to their conversation that Wade recognized. It was the overloud banter of guys trying to outdo each other in order to impress a woman.

Huh? Those guys had known Kim for years, and as far as Wade knew, neither of them had much interest in her. He squinted so he could get a get a closer look at what they were up to—then his head shot up and hit the hood of the car.

He cursed, loud enough to have Kim and the guys turn to stare at him.

Wade strode toward them, shoving his screwdriver into the hands of a gofer as he walked past. Yeah, Kim should look alarmed. What did she think she was playing at?

It took all his willpower to keep his eyes on her face, not to let them drop to what he knew those young jerks were looking at—her curves peeking out the top of her hot-pink T-shirt.

"Boys." He bared his teeth in a smile that had the two guys inching backward. "Don't you have work to do?"

They didn't need to be told twice. With muttered goodbyes to Kim and a couple of last, lingering glances, they disappeared.

Wade grabbed Kim's elbow in a way that he realized must look possessive, but he didn't care. "What the hell are you doing?"

"I *was* having a private conversation," she said, annoyed.

He tightened his grip. "I see you made some progress with your list."

She colored, but held his gaze. "It's been…interesting."

Wade made a noise that was suspiciously like a growl. Kim's eyes widened, then she smiled. It started out uncertain then, as that big-shot brain of hers ticked over, turned knowing in a way that Wade would have said she *didn't* know, not the last time he'd seen her.

"Are you having a Neanderthal moment?" she asked, and now her smile was way more pleased than he liked.

Dammit, could a new bra give her a whole new level of insight, of confidence? His gaze dropped to her T-shirt and he had trouble dragging it away again. How was he supposed to prepare a race car with this kind of distraction?

Maybe he could stow Kim somewhere—away from other men's eyes. He was aware that his urge to send her into seclusion was unreasonable. But although she might be looking around the garage with brazen interest, he knew from their date that she didn't have a lot of experience with men. He wasn't about to stand by and let some guy take advantage of her.

He didn't make the mistake of telling her where he was coming from—unlike his sisters, Kim didn't think he was the fount of all wisdom. Instead, he said, "What are your plans until the race starts?"

"I'm on my way to Justin's motor home. It's time for my dialysis."

Perfect. Wade started walking and tugged her along. "I'll take you."

"I know the way." She tried to shake him off, but he wasn't letting her go. She made a little hiss of annoyance, and he would have bet money the word *Neanderthal* was running through her mind.

There was nothing Neanderthal about a guy protecting his…protecting a woman who didn't necessarily know enough to protect herself.

She could have had the security guard on the owners' and drivers' motor home lot make him stay out, but she didn't. Wade counted that as a small victory.

Justin's motor home was the most distinctive in the lot—the restored 1947 Manor was like a shiny silver bullet among the larger, squarer-built minipalaces in glossy black, green and brown. Kim entered the code into the security touchpad, then opened the door.

"Thanks for the escort." No gratitude in her voice, more like a determination to get inside the motor home and shut the door firmly in Wade's face.

He stuck his foot in the way. "Justin was telling me I should check out his new TV."

"Don't you have a car to set up?"

"It's already been inspected, so we can't do a thing to it. I'm free until the driver's briefing."

"I'd rather you gave me some privacy."

"Is dialysis something you do naked?" he asked, interested.

I WILL NOT BLUSH, I will not blush. To Kim's surprise, her cheeks remained free of the betraying heat. Huh, it made no scientific sense, but she'd somehow convinced herself not to blush. Maybe she could talk her kidneys into resuming normal service, too.

"It's personal," she said to Wade about the dialysis. "If you want to see the TV you can come in, but then you have to leave."

Inside, Wade headed straight to the living area, ignoring the brick-red-and-gray color scheme, the blond wood, the real gray linoleum and the dazzling chrome fittings, in favor of the large, flat screen built into one of the overhead consoles. Trust a jock to think that the most interesting feature of this antique-on-wheels was the brand-new TV set!

Kim hooked a new bag of dialysate fluid onto the coat hook that Justin had installed especially for her, but that was as far as she was going until Wade left. She sat down on the couch. The underwire of her new bra had been digging into her rib cage the last half hour, so she ran a finger under it through the fabric of her T-shirt.

"Does it hurt?" Wade turned back from the TV set.

Her hand froze at her breast.

He laughed out loud. "Not the bra, idiot, the dialysis."

Had he just called one of the finest scientific minds in the South—with potential to be one of the finest in the nation, if she could darn well live long enough—an idiot?

Kim was torn between outrage—no matter that she didn't boast of her intelligence, she was used to other people treating it as something special—and a sudden bubble of hilarity. Hilarity won. She started to chortle.

"That bra is no joke," Wade said, though his eyes gleamed. "Every man at the track had his eyes on you, and wished he had his hands on you, too." He broke off abruptly.

Kim's laughter dried up in the heated silence.

She said tentatively, "*Every* man?"

Wade's eyes didn't leave hers. "Every man," he said huskily as he leaned toward her.

Now he would deliver on that mind-blowing kiss he'd promised. And despite the disappointment of that first embrace, Kim suddenly had no doubt that he would indeed blow her mind. She knew it from the weakness in her limbs, from the heat that radiated through her. She didn't need to kiss him, not for her list, so she should tell him no. But someone must have glued her lips closed—she couldn't say a word.

He lifted a hand, went for the neckline of her T-shirt...and tugged it higher, his fingers brushing the soft flesh there, so that she shivered. "Maybe you should spare us poor guys the agony of temptation," he said.

Then he pulled away.

Huh? What happened to her kiss?

"I've decided to help you with that list of yours," Wade announced, cool and calm, as if he hadn't even thought about locking lips with her.

Kim found her voice. "Thanks, but we already had our date. We kissed. Let's not mess with the magic."

As always, she made him laugh. Kim wasn't used to having someone ride the wave of her sarcastic sense of humor. Usually, it swamped people.

She tried again. "How about we take it on trust that you're capable of that mind-blowing kiss, and never see each other again."

He laughed harder. "This isn't about kissing you, or dating you. It's about helping you out."

"I don't need help. And even if I did, I'm not your responsibility."

He folded his arms. "You think I should tell Hugo your plan to get drunk and go to wild parties, so he can keep an eye on you?"

Kim blanched. "I'm thirty-three years old, I don't need a sitter." She remembered how Wade had been responsible for his father, then his mother, at far too young an age. He obviously had an overdeveloped sense of protectiveness.

But Kim wasn't his family, he had no reason to look after her. Unless, of course, he really liked her. But for some reason he was pretending he didn't want to date her. Her brain, which effortlessly processed the theories of molecular biology, started to hurt.

"But if you want to talk about that kiss..." he said.

"I don't."

"I think it's best to surprise you," he reflected. "If it

happens when you least expect it, it might make it more exciting for you."

"It certainly couldn't be less exciting," she said crossly.

Darn it, he was laughing again.

CHAPTER SEVEN

ISABEL HAD THE FULCRUM Racing sponsor suite, high above the Michigan track, looking just how she liked it. Uniformed catering staff had set up their equipment in the small kitchen area, and had screened their clutter with two floral arrangements. The mostly male guests sat in the banked seating near the front of the room—ten laps into the race, a couple of early passing maneuvers kept them glued to their seats.

She'd made her usual expert assessment of the dozen or so women who'd arrived with their husbands or boyfriends. Five of them were serious fans, so she'd ensured they had good views of the track. A couple were what Isabel privately called "as long as" fans. They'd watch the race with enjoyment, as long as there wasn't a discussion happening about kids, shopping or men. They didn't need much attention. The remainder were women who'd been persuaded to come along by their men, and were either new to NASCAR, so not sure if they liked it, or they'd been before and hadn't found it to their taste. Much as Isabel couldn't understand that last viewpoint, it was her job to make sure they had a good time so that their husbands could, too.

She settled a cluster of them on the leather couches

near the door—no point wasting a good view of the track on them—and instructed an attractive male waiter to keep them supplied with wine, beer and snacks.

Flitting between the various groups, Isabel segued from discussions of lap times and engine blowups to chatter about the hottest racing merchandise, to gossip about which driver was dating which model.

It was hard work, but she was in her element. She loved this; she needed it.

A commotion from the doorway of the suite distracted her from her conversation with the wife of one of the minor sponsor CEOs.

Clay Mortimer was there, with a group of people, and Isabel's assistant, Lisa, hadn't realized who he was. He wasn't on the guest list, having told Isabel he wasn't coming today, and with his shaved head and his worn T-shirt and faded jeans, he looked more like a gate-crasher in search of a free beer than a big-spending corporate sponsor.

Isabel hurried over to sort out the confusion. Clay introduced her to his associates—two men, retail clients of Turn-Rite Tools, and their wives.

"Do you have room for us in here today?" he asked.

"Of course." She wouldn't have refused him if they'd been down to their last bread crust. The wives, Isabel was relieved to see, were already looking out toward the track, and one referred to Justin as a "hottie." One of the men let out a whoop as Justin passed Kent Grosso. None of them needed babysitting, which meant Isabel might have a chance to talk to Clay about the sponsorship.

"Can I get you folks a drink?" With the crook of a finger she summoned a barman. She settled the guests in a prime viewing spot, all the while filling them in on Justin's tenth-place qualifying result, how he was feeling about the car this weekend, who he thought would be hard to beat today. One of the men asked her opinion on a controversial penalty that had been awarded last week, and her understated assessment of who was at fault had them chuckling.

Throughout her almost-monologue, Clay remained silent. When she deemed his clients were happily engrossed in the race, she turned to him—and found him watching her, his blue eyes assessing.

He took a couple of steps backward and indicated she should follow.

"Those are two of my most difficult customers," he said when they were alone. "You have them eating out of your hand."

Isabel gathered his statement was intended to convey approval. She flicked a glance over her shoulder—all four guests were still absorbed. "Thanks, but it's not me, it's NASCAR. It has that effect on people."

He snorted. "Let me guess, this is one of those intangibles you mentioned."

"Exactly. You'll find it's not uncommon for—" She broke off as her brother joined them. Dixon shook hands with Clay, then began explaining some of the finer points of the racing action.

No one was better than Dixon at providing entertaining commentary. But after a few minutes, Clay's attention wandered as he scanned the room. "There are more women in here than I expected," he said abruptly. "Most of them are watching the race."

"NASCAR has a huge female fan base." Dixon

switched with enthusiasm to another aspect of the sport he loved. "Marketers are increasingly finding it a great way to target women."

Isabel winced. She knew just what Clay would say to that.

"Ninety-five percent of the people who use Turn-Rite tools are men."

Bingo.

Dixon shot Isabel an apologetic look as he lapsed into awkward silence. This was why he left sponsorship to her.

"Clay, do you have any idea yet what percentage of Turn-Rite products are purchased as gifts?" she asked.

"Maybe thirty percent," he admitted grudgingly, clearly sensing where she was going.

"That's probably not far off the percentage of NASCAR fans who are female," she said. "And although I don't have numbers, anecdotal evidence suggests that women do by far the majority of gift buying."

He nodded.

"I suspect you'll find, as the previous owners of Turn-Rite did, that NASCAR covers your market in both breadth and depth."

"Is that right?" he said, all irony-laden amazement. A sudden smile transformed his harsh ruggedness, giving it a rough charm that startled Isabel.

Dixon excused himself as Isabel backed up her assertion with talk of the sales spikes Turn-Rite usually saw around Christmas and Father's Day. When Clay didn't comment, she began to estimate what percentage of the total gifts bought for men might be tools. It wasn't the most solid of ground, so she was relieved when Clay interrupted her.

"If I agree that most women prefer to buy their husbands, sons and fathers tools on every gift occasion, and that thanks to Fulcrum Racing, Turn-Rite Tools is their preferred brand, can we change the subject?" he asked.

She felt her cheeks color. "Is this another way of saying I talk too much?"

"It's a way of saying you try too hard."

She bristled. "Turn-Rite Tools' involvement in Fulcrum Racing is important to me. It's worth fighting for."

"Take a tip from me, Isabel, the more important it is, the less you should say. When you're doing your settling-in chitchat—" he jerked his head in the direction of his colleagues "—it's okay to talk until you run out of oxygen." He broke off. "Do you ever get light-headed?"

"I do *not* run out of oxygen," she said. Though in fact, she did sometimes find herself surreptitiously gulping air.

He grinned. "Nothing to be ashamed of, your voice is nice to listen to. But when you have something important to say, you should use the minimum words to get your point across. Sometimes," he added, "it's best to say nothing at all."

Isabel, who had spent most of her life waging war on silence, was appalled at the suggestion. Her feelings must have shown on her face, because Clay laughed.

"If you can't handle saying nothing, change the subject, give the person you're talking to time to process what you said." He paused. "You could ask them something unrelated, like…are you married?"

It took several seconds of expectant, uncomfortable silence for Isabel to realize it was more than abstract advice. Clay was asking her the question.

"I…not anymore," she said. "Are you?"

"Not anymore," he echoed.

There was another of those charged moments between them. As much a warning to herself as to him, Isabel said, "I'm seeing someone."

How on earth had they got here, when she was meant to be selling Clay on the team? She regrouped her thoughts.

"Tell me, Clay," she said, "what would it take for you to commit to retaining Turn-Rite's NASCAR sponsorship?"

"Good question," he said approvingly. "I guess I'd need to feel the money was doing some good."

It was a vague answer for a man so unequivocal. But it was enough for Isabel to see a way ahead. "Justin's doing a hospital visit with kidney transplant patients, sick children, next Wednesday. Why don't you come along?"

Clay frowned. "That's not exactly what I meant."

"Come anyway," she said.

"Will you be there?"

"Absolutely." She hadn't planned to, but someone had to make sure he saw whatever it was he needed in order to feel good about the sponsorship.

"Then so will I," he said.

Satisfied that she had some kind of commitment, Isabel let him watch the race. Justin finished thirteenth after a performance that was solid rather than exciting. Ten minutes after the end, Hugo arrived in the suite for his debrief with Dixon. Isabel had been watching for him.

"Let me introduce you to Justin's crew chief, Hugo Murphy. You didn't get a chance to talk to him last week," she said to Clay. If anyone embodied all that was good and true about NASCAR, it was Hugo.

She introduced the two men. Hugo was every bit as professional toward Clay as Isabel expected. He started to talk about the race, but when he saw Clay wasn't interested in dissecting every lap, he talked tools instead.

Hugo was the perfect match for her, Isabel thought with an inward sigh. Like her, he had an impeccable NASCAR pedigree. With just the tiniest bit of polishing—which she was eminently qualified to supply—he and Isabel would be the ultimate NASCAR double act.

His good looks were an added bonus—he was much better-looking than Clay. Taller than Clay, too. And he had hair… She halted her thoughts. Why was she comparing the two men?

She inched closer to Hugo until her arm brushed his. He moved perceptibly away. Isabel froze.

I'm crowding him, no man likes to be crowded. Her ex-husband had told her that. She held her breath, as if she could take up less space. Beside her, Clay's presence seemed to expand, pushing into her thoughts.

Hugo was now debating the merits of the new Turn-Rite wrench the team was using over the old one. There was only so much you could say about a wrench—Isabel noticed Clay's eyes starting to glaze over at the same time as Hugo did.

"Hugo, I was telling Clay last week what a difference Wade Abraham has made to the team this season. But I'm sure you'd do a better job than I of explaining the car chief role."

"Of course." Hugo launched into an explanation.

Isabel kept her eyes glued to him, let the words he spoke from his long NASCAR experience soothe her.

At last, Hugo excused himself to talk to Dixon. She watched him go.

"If he's the someone you're seeing," Clay said with what was becoming a familiar, unwelcome bluntness, "you have a problem."

"I have no idea what you mean," she said coolly.

Clay shrugged. "I'm a good judge of people—that's how I made a lot of money without much of an education. That, and not wasting time on a road that's going nowhere. Take it from me, the crew chief guy isn't interested in you." His eyes flicked over her, then suddenly he cracked a wide, appreciative grin that took ten years off his appearance and put mischief in his eyes. "Leastways, not in more than a roll in the hay, and I'll bet every man in this room would be interested in that."

The words were balm to her ego—and salt in the wound of Hugo's neglect. "Is that your idea of a compliment?" she said stiffly.

"Nope." Now his gaze openly appraised her, from top to toe. "I just tell it like I see it."

Isabel ignored the trickle of excitement down her spine. "I'd rather not hear your opinions on my personal life. All I want is a fair chance to put the case for Turn-Rite Tools' NASCAR sponsorship, starting with a visit to the hospital with Justin next week."

"You've got it," he said. "But I'm warning you, I'm about as enthusiastic about this sponsorship deal as that crew chief guy is about whatever he has going with you."

Isabel was momentarily winded, unable to say which potential loss terrified her the most—the sponsorship or

Hugo. Mustering the remnants of her dignity, she said, "In that case, it looks like we'll be just fine."

WADE, RACHEL AND JUSTIN met in Hugo's office for their Tuesday morning debrief. Justin's thirteenth-place finish at Michigan wasn't bad, but with only three more races left to qualify among the twelve drivers who would race the Chase for the NASCAR Sprint Cup, they couldn't afford to slip any lower. Only the drivers who made the Chase were eligible to win the NASCAR Sprint Cup Series championship.

Hugo's debriefs always followed the same pattern. Compliments first, then complaints. Today, he started with Rachel.

"You got great power out of that engine," he said. "Kent Grosso was flying, but Justin still got past him. I wouldn't mind betting we were producing more horsepower than anyone." He nodded approvingly at Rachel.

"Thanks, Hugo."

He turned to Wade. "You made a good call, going with a two-tire change at the final pit stop. The car stuck to the track just fine, and if we'd changed all four Justin would have finished farther back."

Wade nodded. Hugo then commended Justin on the way he'd negotiated his way around a couple of multicar pileups.

Then it was time for complaints. Rachel got a tellingoff over fuel consumption, which had been higher than normal. Justin's fuel cell had needed filling ten laps from the end of the race, rather than just a splash of gas to see them through. They'd lost valuable fractions of a second.

"The guys took the trackbar up too far when we pitted

during the yellow flag," Hugo told Wade next. "We struggled in Turn Three through to the next pit stop."

"I made the wrong call," Wade agreed.

Hugo nodded, satisfied with Wade's accountability, then turned to Justin. "We have to do something about the way you're going into the turns. You're all over the place."

It was an exaggeration, but Justin had struggled to handle the car entering the turns for a couple of months now.

"The car's too loose," Justin said. "I keep telling the guys."

"Tightening it doesn't seem to work," Hugo pointed out. "It's particularly frustrating given that, thanks to Rachel, the engine's been performing so much better the last few months."

Rachel murmured heartfelt agreement.

Hugo leaned back in his chair. "Let's brainstorm how we can tackle this. I want to see an improvement at Bristol."

Wade was pretty sure he had a handle on the problem. Normally, he would jump in and say what needed to be done, then be prepared to argue until he got his way.

But maybe Kim's more considered approach to life was rubbing off on him, because today he waited until Rachel and Justin had thrown their suggestions into the ring.

"Wade?" Hugo looked expectantly at him.

"This has been happening since Rachel took over as engine builder," Wade said. He heard Rachel's sharp intake of breath as she anticipated an attack on her skills. "She's done such a good job, I think our engines are actually too good."

Rachel looked mollified, but suspicious.

"You think the horsepower is the problem?" Hugo asked.

Wade nodded. "We need to make less horsepower going into the turns. Justin's staying on the throttle too long and losing control of the back of the car. He has trouble correcting that himself, so we need to fix it at the engine level."

Wade deliberately didn't say any more, though he could have. Because for all that horsepower was measured in numbers, it was an emotive issue. Some people thought there was no such thing as too much horsepower. Wade wasn't one of them. Some drivers handled excess horsepower just fine—other times, you hindered a guy by giving him a car that was too powerful.

Hugo made a few notes on the pad in front of him. Then he looked up. "I think Wade has a point," he said addressing the entire table. "Rachel, this weekend I'd like you to take it down a bit in the turns."

Rachel didn't look happy. But she agreed.

Hugo asked Wade to stay behind after she and Justin left. He put the cap back on his pen, signaling this was personal, not business. "How's Kim?"

"She seemed okay at Michigan." Wade frowned. "Haven't you spoken to her?"

"I've been busy," Hugo said, "and she won't tell me anything when I do call."

"I told her I'll help her out with a few things." He wasn't happy that he felt so protective toward Kim, but for his own peace of mind, he couldn't ignore it. The sooner they got through her list, the sooner he could put her out of his mind.

Hugo raised his eyebrows. "What things?"

"Just some stuff she wants to get done."

"You mean those shelves she wants in her den? I told her I could do that."

"She didn't exactly jump at the idea," Wade said without correcting Hugo's assumption about the assistance he was providing. "But it'll mean I can keep an eye on her for you."

"You're damned stubborn," Hugo agreed. For the first time, his regular complaint sounded like a compliment.

KIM FINISHED THE FINAL read-through of her report on the project that had consumed her time for the last six months. With a murmur of satisfaction, she clicked to send the file to the lab's printing department. By tomorrow, she would have bound copies ready to distribute for peer review.

She ran a hand around the back of her neck, then stretched out her arms, aware that even her desk job took more out of her physically than it used to.

She glanced at her watch. Four o'clock, and she hadn't yet gotten around to making the phone call that had been top of her to-do list today.

She dialed Hugo's direct line at the team headquarters.

"Are you okay?" Hugo's first response to a phone call from her these days was that it was a medical emergency. Which meant Kim called him even less than she used to.

"I'm fine, Dad. Uh, what have you been up to?" She never asked her father for things for herself, so she didn't quite know where to start asking for Rachel.

"The usual," Hugo said. "Team debrief this morning, working lunch with Dixon, paperwork…"

Kim saw a foothold and latched on. "I'll bet Rachel got some kudos in the team meeting."

"She did, but so did the others."

"Rachel's come along so fast since she was promoted," Kim said. Hugo agreed, so she added, "She'd make a wonderful crew chief."

Instantly, guilt assailed her. It took her a moment to identify it: she felt as if she were betraying Wade!

That's crazy.

"I know she has the personal qualities," Hugo said.

Kim swallowed. "And—" she had to force the words out "—the technical skill. Rachel hangs out with the mechanics so much, she knows the whole car."

"You're right," Hugo said thoughtfully.

She had more to say, but instead, she mumbled, "I'd better get back to work, Dad. I'll call you later in the week."

She dropped the phone back onto its cradle as if it had stung her. What was wrong with her?

Then Wade's voice said, "Hey," from her office doorway. She jumped sky-high.

She hadn't seen him since he'd left her in Justin's motor home at Michigan. But she'd been thinking about his insistence that he would help her achieve the goals on her list. Although she didn't want his help, she could admit it was a generous offer—she knew just how busy a car chief was in the middle of the NASCAR Sprint Cup Series season. Was that why she felt bad about talking to her dad about Rachel?

"How did you get in here?" She frowned so she wouldn't look guilty. "This is a secure area."

He strolled in, tall and gorgeous in boots, jeans and

a dark orange T-shirt. "I told the receptionist I'm your boyfriend, and she pointed me in this direction."

No doubt Janey had been speechless, Kim thought as she removed her reading glasses and slipped them into a drawer. Who would believe that a hunk like Wade, a man who positively vibrated with energy and charisma, would be dating Kim?

The thought that her personal babe quotient had rocketed a thousand percent in her colleagues' eyes was rather pleasing. "But you're not my boyfriend."

He perched on the edge of her desk. "Just say the word," he said.

Had he just suggested…? Kim leaned back so she wasn't quite so close to his tantalizing presence, and unscrambled her thoughts. She realized he wore a guarded, slightly shell-shocked expression.

She breathed again. "You weren't actually offering to be my boyfriend just then, were you?"

"Ah…" he said cautiously.

"I ought to take you up on that, just to teach you a lesson about lying to my colleagues."

"Sorry," he said without a trace of apology. "I didn't think they'd let me in if I told them I was here to take you to get a tattoo."

"What?" Kim squawked.

"It's on the list." As if she'd forgotten. "And if you're going to get drunk and go to wild parties, it makes sense to do the tattoo next. It'll help your street cred."

"I don't *have* any street cred."

He scanned her navy blue suit jacket and high-collared blouse, her hair held back by a pale blue Alice band. "True."

She glared at him—her clothes were perfectly acceptable in her job. "Or should I say, I don't *want* street cred."

"If that's so, you wouldn't have put the tattoo on your list," he suggested.

Unfortunately, he was right. "I need to think about this some more," she hedged.

"Of course you do," he said. "Say, for another fifteen years?"

Sounded good to Kim.

"Uh-uh." He read her mind, wagged a finger at her. "The decision to get a tattoo can never be part of a serious thought process. It has to be spontaneous."

"Is that because when people think about it they back out?" she asked.

His grin told her she'd hit the mark. He pushed a stack of papers across the desk toward her, disordering it. "Pack up this stuff and we'll go."

"Quit rushing me," she complained.

He rolled his eyes. "Anything faster than glacier-pace is rushing, as far as you're concerned."

"I'm *sensible*," she said. "So shoot me."

"You want to do the things on your list, right?"

"Ye-es." Darn it, she was even talking at glacier-pace now. "I can organize my own tattoo."

"You shouldn't have to suffer alone."

She shivered. "You think it'll hurt?"

He eyed her as if he was unsure how much bad news she could take. "Some."

"How much?" she demanded.

"Enough that you'll need someone to kiss it better."

Heat arced through the air between them, so hot that Kim thought the papers on her desk might vaporize. "I thought you said this—you helping me—isn't about dating."

He smirked. "It would be like the Kiss of Life—purely medicinal."

"Not mind-blowing, then," she said, half relieved, half disappointed.

"Probably not."

Aware that she was, as ever, hopelessly out of her depth, but for the first time in her life unable to do the sensible thing and swim for shore, she lifted her eyebrows to convey her doubts as to the existence of his famous mind-blowing kiss.

He grinned. "Are you ready to go?"

WALKING THROUGH THE STARK white corridors of Booth Laboratories with Wade at her side was a nerve-wracking experience. Yes, Kim enjoyed the respectfully envious glances of a couple of the admin staff. But when one of her senior colleagues, Dr. Phil Warren, stopped her to ask a question, she felt compelled to introduce him to Wade. She'd dated Phil a couple of times before the relationship fizzled out through lack of interest. Now, she spent the entire conversation worrying that Phil, who tended toward pomposity, would make a fool out of Wade.

Wade asked Phil a few questions about his work, and then Phil returned the compliment by asking how the NASCAR Sprint Cup Series season was going so far. Wade gave him a brief summary.

"I went to a NASCAR race once," Phil said. Kim had taken him along to a race here in Charlotte. "Did you know they get nearly two hundred thousand people at the track?"

Wade admitted he did know.

"The cars had changed since I last saw a race," Phil confided. "They used to have those long-nosed things that sit right down low on those enormous wheels. These days, they look more like regular cars." He nodded at Wade. "That's progress, I guess."

"I guess." Wade shook Phil's hand.

To think Kim had been worried about Phil making a fool of Wade! She clenched her jaw to keep from laughing as she led him out of the building, but she was snickering by the time they hit the parking lot.

"You are such a NASCAR snob," Wade chided her. She heard the rumble of laughter in his voice. "Anyone could get a stock car confused with an Indy car."

"Anyone," she agreed, and her snicker turned into a full-on laugh at the memory of Phil's knowledgeable earnestness.

"That's harsh, Kim," Wade said. "Poor old Phil." But his voice shook on the last word, and then he was laughing along with her.

It felt wonderfully carefree, Kim thought, to let their mirth fly on the late summer breeze.

"We'll take my car," Wade said when he sobered up. He gestured to the red Mustang that way out-styled the family sedans in the Booth Laboratories parking lot. "I'll drop you back to your car later." He paused. "If you're not in too much pain."

He was joking, Kim decided. Thousands of people had tattoos. No one would do it if it really hurt.

CHAPTER EIGHT

MATT'S TATTS WAS A respectable-looking studio in Arbor Street, in Charlotte's bohemian NoDa district. Matt was an enormous man, elaborately tattooed up both arms. The design disappeared inside his muscle shirt, then emerged around his neck, a colorful, abstract pattern that Kim considered almost a work of art.

In response to Kim's questions, he outlined the costs and the procedure. "You want to choose a design?" he asked.

"Just a moment," Kim said. She grabbed Wade's arm, tugged him aside.

"I think we should shop around," she murmured. "This is the first place we've been. There might be somewhere better."

"Hmm." Wade pursed his lips. "This place was recommended by a couple of guys I know."

"It's a good idea to comparison shop," she said virtuously.

"No," Wade said. Without waiting to hear Kim's full justification as to why she should spend a week or two shopping around, Wade took her back to Matt. "We'd like to look at the designs," he said.

Pushy jock!

Matt sat them down with a folder that had plastic sleeves filled with tattoo designs. "Let me know when you've figured out what you want." His gaze flicked over Kim. "And where you want it."

"Where will it be least painful?" Wade asked, and Kim briefly forgave him.

Matt rubbed his chin. "Somewhere with a bit of padding is best." He glanced at Kim again. "It's hard to say how much it'll hurt, because people feel it differently. But you might want to avoid anywhere that's directly over a bone—the back of your hand, or your ankle will hurt more than, say, your upper arm."

"So the least painful place would be Kim's derriere," Wade suggested. Kim's head jerked around.

Matt nodded. "Yep, the cheeks are pretty popular."

Kim buried her face in the design folder. Was she really sitting here while two men discussed her bottom? She'd give anything for a meaty conversation about oncogenes.

"How long will the tattoo take?" She interrupted them before they could get to even more personal body parts.

"Something small with a couple of different colors, like a flower…maybe an hour. Something like that—" he pointed to a picture on the wall of a jewel-scaled dragon coiled around a tower "—a couple of weeks."

"I'll go for small," she said hastily. "*Very* small. Do you have anything tiny?"

"Maybe you'd like Matt to use one of the new invisible inks," Wade suggested.

"Yes!" She practically squealed the word in her excitement. "Invisible would be perfect. I could have

Justin's car number, 448." Then she realized Matt looked confused…and Wade was laughing.

"You creep! You…you—" she cast around for something to throw and chose a pen from the table in front of her "—you cretin!"

The pen fell short, and Wade swooped to catch it before it hit the ground. "We have *got* to teach you to throw," he said, still laughing. "That's the third time you've demonstrated your pathetic right arm."

"It would be perfectly possible to have invisible ink tattoos," she informed him crossly. "Ones you could only see under ultraviolet light, for example."

"Of course it's possible," he soothed her. "But not today."

Kim pffed. "And leave my right arm out of it," she muttered. "We can't all be jocks. Some of us have to save the world." She stuck her nose in the air, held the catalogue up to her face.

She saw it immediately, the perfect design.

"This one." She turned the folder around, pointed at the red-and-orange butterfly. "It's like a symbol of freedom and lightheartedness. I'll have it on my thigh."

Where it wouldn't show all the time, but she could choose to reveal it when she wore shorts or a swimsuit.

"You wanna think about it?" Matt asked. "Some people change their minds."

About to grab the opportunity to delay, Kim caught Wade's eye. Darn it, he expected her to renege. "I want to go ahead," she said.

"Kim, are you sure?" *Now* Wade chose to get concerned.

"I'm certain," she lied.

HALF AN HOUR LATER, Kim stepped back into the reception area, trying not to limp. Wade dropped the car magazine he'd been thumbing through and stood. "That was quick. You okay?"

"Fine." Her jaw was sore from being clenched.

"I didn't hear any screaming," he said.

"She was stoic," Matt told him.

Kim looked at him in surprise—she'd whimpered pretty much the whole way through. Matt winked.

Wade caught the exchange, and moved closer to Kim. "Let's go. I bought steaks—I'll cook dinner."

Her leg hurt and a wave of fatigue had just washed over her. Kim couldn't think of any good reason not to yield.

WADE'S HOME WASN'T BIG, but the simplicity of the Arts and Crafts style made it feel spacious. The furnishings were in keeping with the house, and Kim found it restful.

She perched on a stool at the kitchen's rustic pine island and watched Wade set two enormous steaks to marinate in soy sauce, honey and chili flakes. Next, he scrubbed two potatoes, rubbed them with oil, wrapped foil around them and put them in the oven.

"I'll tear the lettuce, while you slice the scallions and tomatoes for a salad," he said.

When the potatoes were almost cooked, Wade barbecued the steaks. It was lucky she liked hers medium rare, Kim thought, because he didn't ask, just cooked hers the same length of time he did his own, and slid them onto two plates.

They ate in the dining room, cozy with lead light windows and polished wooden floorboards warmed by a chocolate-brown, deep pile rug. Wade asked Kim about her work, and this time she managed not to insult his quick intelligence. Later, she brought the conversation back to NASCAR, to Justin's odds of making the Chase for the NASCAR Sprint Cup.

"He has a good chance," Wade said. "But he needs to go with his gut more often."

"Don't let Dad hear you say that," Kim said. "He likes to plan the race as much as he can."

"That's fine when things are going as expected. But Justin needs to think faster when everything goes belly-up and the plan doesn't fit anymore."

By the time they'd finished eating, they'd solved every problem Justin had ever encountered in his driving.

Kim helped Wade clear away, but he insisted the dishes could wait until after she'd left.

"There's something I'd rather do," he said.

More than once during the meal her mind had wandered to the promised kiss. Kim moistened her lips with her tongue. Wade obviously felt he had something to prove; she might as well accept the inevitable. She let him take her hand, lead her to the living room.

"I want to see your tattoo," he said, as she sat down on the dark red couch designed along the same clean lines as the house.

That was what he'd rather do? "It's not that interesting," Kim said.

"Someone has to be first," Wade said. "So that you can act as if it's old news when other people see it."

Now that made sense. Her hand went to her thigh. "You're not allowed to laugh," she warned.

He settled beside her. She bunched the fabric of her skirt in her fingers.

"Show," he said. He caught her hand in his, and Kim's fingers tingled.

She hitched her skirt a little higher, and Wade's hand fell away. His eyes were on her bare legs, as if they were the most exciting thing he'd seen since Justin won at Indy.

She inched the fabric over the tattoo. There it was, a small, perfect, red heart. Or more accurately, half a heart. She felt a thrill of pride as she looked at it.

Wade's eyebrows drew together. "Where's the butterfly?"

"I, uh, decided not to get the butterfly," she said.

"You didn't want an image of freedom and light-heartedness?"

Who'd have thought he was listening so hard? "I changed my mind."

A slow, devilishly handsome smile spread across his face. "You chickened out."

"I did not."

He folded his arms, stared her down.

"Okay, I did," she admitted. "Wade, the whole thing was agony. I never dreamed it would hurt so much when I've had so many medical tests that didn't bother me. By the time Matt had outlined one wing, I knew a whole butterfly would kill me. I asked him to turn it into half a heart."

Wade's brows knitted. "You should have told me it was hurting, I'd have taken you out of there."

"I wanted to go through with it—and I was sort of getting used to it by the time he stopped. I may go back and upgrade to the butterfly later," she said without conviction. "Or at least get the rest of the heart."

He tucked a strand of hair behind her ear. "Poor baby, you need something to take your mind off the pain." He pulled her against him, one arm wrapped around her shoulders.

"The pain's not so bad now," she said, her voice muffled against his chest.

"Uh-uh," he chided, one hand stroking her hair. "You don't get over *agony* that fast."

"Maybe agony was an exaggeration." What felt more like agony was being this close to him.

As if he read her thoughts, he moved away. But only so he could twist to face her on the couch. His hands closed around her upper arms. "It's time for me to blow your mind."

His intent, dark gaze alighted on her mouth.

"My mind is unusually strong," she reminded him. "It would take a truly exceptional kiss to blow it."

His dark eyes lit with challenge. The time for words was past.

Wade enfolded Kim in an embrace that was at once gentle and demanding. She couldn't move. She didn't want to move.

His lips met hers and from the moment of contact this bore no resemblance to that first chaste kiss. His mouth was hot, claiming hers with a possessiveness that stunned her. She was no match for his insistence—her lips parted instantly to admit him. There, he tested, teased, tasted. His arms tightened around her, and Kim managed to extricate hers so she could wind them around his neck.

His rock-hard chest reminded her of his superior strength. Yet when Kim sighed against his mouth, she felt his whole body tremble with the same longing that had her in its thrall. It was heady, powerful, intoxicating.

Wade's hands moved down her back, pulling her closer to him. Everything about him was strong male, and he felt so good she wanted to weep.

He eased her gently into the softness of the couch, so that he was on top of her. His hands moved to the buttons of her blouse, and Kim almost shrieked at the sensation of his knuckles grazing her curves.

If she didn't stop him now, they would make love.

"Wade." She pressed her hands to the muscular expanse of his chest, and pushed.

He lifted his mouth from hers. "What is it, baby?"

"Um, you've officially blown my mind, so you can stop now."

His whole body lifted. "You're kidding, right?"

She wriggled beneath him. Bad move, it set up all kinds of reactions within her, and did the same to him, going by the clenching of his jaw. "I mean it. This can't go any further."

She wouldn't have a casual sexual relationship. And even if Wade was interested in something more serious, she hadn't been totally honest about her illness and her chances of a transplant. They couldn't have a relationship based on deceit. Not ready to tell him that truth, she wrapped her arms around herself. "I'm sorry."

WADE WANTED TO HOWL with frustration. But Kim looked so anxious, her lips clamped together so hard they'd turned pale, he reined in his resentment. Maybe he could assuage her fears, and they could get back to what they were doing. "I don't do one-night stands, if that's what you're worried about." One night with Kim would never be enough anyway—just one taste of her told him that.

She shook her head. "Maybe we could be friends. Just for now."

Unconsciously, her fingers walked across his chest. That light pressure through the knit of his shirt was enough to ratchet up his desire for her yet another notch.

He captured her hand. "Friends don't do that," he said roughly. "Dammit, Kim, I didn't imagine your response just now."

She blushed. "I'm not ready to make love with you."

Wade sat up so Kim could do the same. She retucked her blouse, and Wade got a glimpse of smooth, pale midriff. "When you will be ready?" he said, frustrated. "Let me guess, about fifteen years' time?"

"I…no…sooner than that," she blurted, her color deepening.

That was something, he supposed.

"Besides," she said, "you may not want to rush into it, either."

"Believe me, I planned to take it very, very slowly," he said, and saw longing flare in her eyes.

Awkwardly, she dipped her head to put on her sandals. Her feet were as sexy as the rest of her, Wade noticed. Long and slim, with high arches.

"I meant," she said, her voice muffled, "if you and I are dating, my dad's bound to find out. You need to figure out if you want to mix work and pleasure."

Hell! Wade had been so caught up in wanting her,

he hadn't even thought about his job. About the promotion he wanted.

Kim was gorgeous, she kissed like a dream, and she'd been incredibly cute about that silly tattoo. And they had a major chemistry thing going. But were a few weeks or months of dating worth risking his dream for?

No way.

Wade eased away from her on the couch, ran a hand around the back of his neck. "I guess you're right, we shouldn't rush things. Friends is good."

She looked slightly disappointed. "For now," she prompted him.

"Yeah, for now." For always. He couldn't screw up the crew chief job, not even for her.

She leaned over and kissed his cheek. The brush of her curves against his arm produced a physical reaction that had nothing platonic to it. Carefully, he recreated the space between them.

"I'd better get you home," he said.

Then he had to figure out a way to extricate himself from this mess.

He couldn't date her, that was obvious. And he couldn't in all honesty call himself her friend—not when he planned to report back to Hugo about her health.

He needed to get back to his goal: get the crew chief job. If he could maybe help Kim out a little on the way, take care of her, then that was a good thing. But that was all.

He glanced at the date on his watch. Hugo had said Dixon would announce the new crew chief after the race at Richmond—less than two weeks away.

All Wade had to do was keep his "friendship" with

Kim going for a couple more weeks and keep Hugo informed about her condition. He could help Kim through the rest of her list in that time, which meant he'd be doing her a favor.

Then, after the announcement was made… If Wade got the job, he would have even less time for a serious relationship. His relationship with Kim, whatever they called it, would wane naturally. Without Kim ever knowing that Wade had used her.

FRIENDS! KIM GROANED INTO her tea glass, and the sound echoed back out at her.

What the heck had she been thinking, when what she really wanted was to tear off Wade's clothes and hers, and make love?

He'd accused her of chickening out of the butterfly tattoo and he'd been right. But suggesting they be friends had been so namby-pamby, she'd be lucky if the chickens would let her back in the henhouse.

She was…whatever the least courageous life-form was. Someone at work would probably know.

Wade would probably know. The more she talked to him, the more she realized he was well-read and that he used his learning to good effect. Yet another thing she liked about him.

Kim swallowed the last of her tea and reached over the back of the couch, where she lay hooked up to her dialysate, to deposit her glass on the sideboard. Then she picked up the phone and dialed Dr. Peterson. She'd felt so much better the last couple of weeks, she was certain things must have improved. She'd asked the doctor to run more tests.

Because if she was going to be honest with Wade, she needed to know exactly how much better she was.

The receptionist put her through to Dr. Peterson.

"Kim, how are you?"

"You probably know the answer to that better than I do." She laughed, nervous.

"You're right, I do." There was no answering humor in his voice.

Kim gripped the phone tighter. "How do the tests look?"

"Kim, I'm sorry," he said heavily. "There's no improvement. In fact, there's been a tiny decline in your residual kidney function."

"I can't believe it," she protested. "I've felt so good."

"Maybe you've made some lifestyle changes that have had a positive effect on your frame of mind. But the numbers—" she heard the shrug in his voice "—don't lie."

Kim stayed silent.

"You know this doesn't get better of its own accord," he said gently. "You of all people understand that."

She processed the implications of what he was telling her. Then tried to deny them. Again.

Damn.

She felt a stinging on her cheeks and when she touched her fingers to them, found dampness. She was crying.

Stupid, she admonished herself. Tears were just an overflow of the lachrymal glands, they couldn't change anything.

"Kim, have you talked to your father yet?"

She cleared her throat. "I do plan to tell someone. Maybe not my father."

After she ended the call, she sat, very still, for a long time. Thinking about how Wade would react if she told him.

Wade was a good man—look at the way he cared for his family. More importantly, although he could have his pick of gorgeous, fun women, he chose to spend his time with Kim.

He wanted to make love with her. And she'd implied that they would, soon.

It was time to be honest with him.

So she would call him and say she planned to arrive in Bristol Wednesday night. If he suggested they get together on Thursday, she would go ahead.

Go ahead and trust him more than she'd ever trusted anyone.

Kim pressed back into the cushions. He might not want her anymore, of course. But in that case, it was best she knew now, before she did something crazy like fall in love with him.

Which didn't actually sound that crazy.

"I might fall in love with him," she said out loud. Okay, now it sounded stupid. She hardly knew him, and she'd spent most of their time together sparring with him. And yet…

ISABEL HALF EXPECTED Clay wouldn't show up at the hospital on Wednesday. But when she walked into the hospital reception, he was there. He must have come from his office, for he wore a suit, obviously expensive, charcoal-gray with a pinstripe over a white shirt and light gray tie. But the finery couldn't disguise his fighter's stance, the stubborn thrust of his chin.

Isabel hadn't spoken to him since the race at Michigan. She told herself it was because he'd suggested the less she said the more effective she'd be…but that was a convenient excuse. She was too disturbed by their last conversation. Despite her anger over what he'd said about Hugo, she couldn't stop thinking about the frankly sensual appraisal in his gaze.

Though right now, he looked merely businesslike, and she wondered if she could have imagined it.

She greeted Clay, ran through the morning's agenda before he could start any kind of personal conversation. But it seemed he was all business today—in the lull before Justin arrived, his questions were confined to the sponsorship agreement. The phrase "roll in the hay" didn't feature.

Justin breezed in a couple of minutes late. The hospital administrator who was managing his visit got excited almost to the point of losing her voice, but Justin's charm soon had her relaxing.

They headed to the pediatric kidney ward, where Justin would visit a couple of dozen patients. It was draining work, but Isabel knew he gave his time willingly, and his natural sympathy always made him a favorite for this kind of thing.

Clay and Isabel hung back while Justin shook hands with each patient, talked to them about their condition, answered their questions about NASCAR—and was entirely gracious if they named some other driver as their favorite.

At one stage, as one little girl told Justin matter-of-factly that if she didn't get a transplant within six months, she would probably die, Isabel wiped a tear from her eye. And realized Clay was doing the same. It was a shock, to see such a tough-looking man affected by the little girl's plight.

"Justin does a great job, doesn't he?" she asked Clay.

Clay cleared his throat. "Yeah."

"You can see that NASCAR gives a lot of people real hope—something to focus on when all around them life is descending into chaos or despair." It did the same for her.

Clay didn't say anything, and she resisted the temptation to go on and on.

But as the tour ended, she ventured the question that was burning a hole in her tongue. "Is this the kind of thing you meant, when you said you would need to see that your NASCAR sponsorship was doing good?"

Behind them, she could hear Justin saying goodbye to the staff. Clay held the swing door at the end of the ward open for her to step out into the elevator bay. "Yes…and no."

"What does that mean?"

He thumbed the elevator button. "Justin's doing good work here, but this isn't where most of Turn-Rite's money goes. If we have enough money for an indulgence like a NASCAR sponsorship, I'd rather put it into something I care a lot about, something where every dollar we put in goes directly to the cause."

"We're not asking for your charity," she said, shocked. "We're asking for a marketing investment that will produce a return, just like any other investment. Continuing to invest in NASCAR will help you make money that you can then give to your good cause. Hospital visits like this one are the icing on the cake."

"The 'cake' is millions of dollars that could be put to a better use," he pointed out. "Isabel, you need to know that every spare dollar my companies make goes to a charitable foundation for cardiac research. That's what I care about. That's *all* I care about."

The elevator arrived, and they stepped into it. Isabel had the awful sensation that the next words out of Clay's mouth would be an announcement that he was dropping the sponsorship. When he reached to press the button for the first floor, she grabbed his hand.

It felt even stronger than that first day she'd shaken it, but maybe, somehow, not as rough. "You promised your decision would take all the facts and figures into account," she said. "Now you're suggesting you'll make up your mind on the basis of some existing policy."

"Maybe I shouldn't have made that promise." His eyes met hers, troubled. "I'm not sure why I did."

"I'm holding you to it," she said fiercely. "You promised to crunch the numbers."

"And I will."

"I need a week," she insisted. "I'll present my business case to you this time next week, in my office."

There was no reason for him to agree with her peremptory demand, but she hoped he would respect her intention to fight. The elevator pinged its arrival at the first floor, and the doors slid open.

Clay said, "I'll see you next week."

Isabel sagged against the back of the elevator after he left. She'd convinced him to read her bulletproof business case. Now she just had to create it.

CHAPTER NINE

JUSTIN DREW THE FIRST qualifying slot on Thursday at Bristol, which he wasn't happy about—it was a cold day, and he'd have preferred to qualify later when the track had warmed up a little. But Kim was thrilled. Wade had asked her to spend the rest of the day with him. Today, at the end of the day, she would tell him.

He collected her from Justin's motor home at two o'clock. He didn't kiss her when she opened the door, which was disappointing. Until he told her what he had planned for the afternoon.

"We're going to the movies," he said, "and we're sitting in the back row."

Make out at the movies.

"That's a terrific idea," she said happily, overlooking the oddly brusque way he'd announced his intention, on the assumption he was still operating in car chief mode.

He took her hand and set off across the infield at a rapid clip. Kim just about had to jog to keep up.

"Slow down," she puffed. "We geniuses aren't as fit as you jocks."

He stopped, and she jogged right into him. He steadied her with his hands on her upper arms, and the contact zinged through her.

"I'm, uh, more mentally agile, of course," she said, her breathlessness nothing to do with her lack of fitness.

"Of course." His gaze lighted on her mouth. Kim saw the longing in his eyes…and saw him decide not to act on it.

"You know—" she swayed toward him, just a fraction "—we don't have to wait until the movie to make out."

With a half laugh, half groan, he lowered his mouth to hers.

The kiss was sweet, tender…and interrupted.

A YOUNG BOY'S voice said loudly behind Wade, "Look, Mommy, Uncle Wade and that lady are k-i-s-s-i-n-g."

Wade stopped k-i-s-s-i-n-g Kim, and cursed under his breath. "Don't tell me…"

Yep. It appeared his entire family was heading toward him, his nephew Marco leading the charge. Marco's mother, Wade's sister Cara, was close behind. Cara's husband didn't appear to be there, but just about everyone else was.

"Surprise!" Cara said. "We brought a picnic." She hugged him, and the rest of them did, too, pulling him into varying degrees of smothering embrace. His mom waited to go last. She squeezed his cheeks the way she'd been doing since he was boy—it was incredibly irritating, not to mention painful, but also a comforting reminder of her unchanging love for him.

"Hi, Mom." Wade dropped a kiss on the striking swathe of silver that ran through her dark hair.

"You didn't call, so I tried your cell, but you didn't answer," she said, no reproach in her voice. "I know you don't make time to eat when you're at the track, so we've brought lunch to you."

Wade usually visited his folks when he was in Bristol, but he'd been so busy thinking about how he could finish off Kim's list, tie up all the loose ends before Richmond, that he hadn't had time even to phone his mom.

His mother looked up at him and tilted her head to one side. "You need to introduce us to your friend."

Kim, understandably, was hanging back, bemused by the noisy Abraham tribe.

"Guys, this is Kim Murphy," he announced. He laced his fingers through hers, tugged her to him. Silence fell. Every member of Wade's family was looking at their joined hands. Heck, anyone would think he'd never dated before!

He realized he never introduced his dates to his family. But Kim wasn't a date—even though he planned to make out at the movies with her today—and he wouldn't have introduced her if his family hadn't ambushed him.

"Kim, meet my nosy, noisy family," he said. He ruffled his nephew's hair. "This is Marco, who, as you'll have gathered, is the spelling champion of the first grade. And this is my mom, Rosa Abraham." He introduced her quickly to everyone else.

His mother's gaze raked her, and there was approval in her voice as she said, "If you and Kim have plans, we can picnic another day. Or maybe Kim could join us?"

Wade was damned if he did, damned if he didn't. He'd never blown his family off before, not for anything, so if he went ahead with his plan to take Kim to the movies, they'd be talking wedding dates. If he took Kim to the picnic, she might get the wrong idea about his intentions.

He decided that was the lesser of the two evils. After Richmond, he and Kim would be over—but he'd have to live with his family's overreaction forever.

THEY PICNICKED on the infield, which was nowhere near as busy as it would be later when the fans started to arrive en masse.

Kim was handed a plate loaded with more food than she could possibly eat. It looked, smelled and tasted delicious—despite the all-American feel of the gathering, the Abrahams obviously held several Lebanese dishes among their family favorites.

While she was disappointed that she wasn't right now making out with Wade in a movie theater, she was intrigued to have this chance to meet his family.

The Abrahams were very friendly, but almost overwhelming in their intensity. Kim was content to sit back and listen to the chatter around her. As she did, it dawned on her that Wade's sisters' conversation, and to a lesser extent his mother's and his brother's, wasn't just social chat. With varying degrees of subtlety, they were sharing their problems, enlisting his support, asking his advice. It was almost, but not quite, badgering. Wade dispensed orders and suggestions like a feudal king whose subjects had sought an audience.

When he was asked to adjudicate in an argument between his brother and his youngest sister, Sarah, Kim almost laughed.

Rosa caught her smile. "Wade is wonderful with his siblings. They adore him."

"It looks to be mutual," Kim said. "It must be great to have such a large family."

"It's a blessing," Rosa said simply. She snapped the lid off a large plastic container. "Time for dessert," she announced. The sweet almond-and-honey scent of baklava wafted toward Kim. She looked at Wade, found him watching her, his eyes inscrutable.

Everyone gathered around Rosa in search of baklava. Sarah, Wade's younger sister, brought Kim a piece of the dessert. Kim tasted it, let the sweet filo pastry dissolve on her tongue.

"So, how long have you been dating Wade?" Sarah asked.

Kim chewed very slowly. "We're not dating." Yet.

Sarah's face fell. "So you can't help me convince my pigheaded brother to lighten up on my boyfriend?"

"Um, I don't think so." Kim licked her spoon, this stuff was so good. "Who's your boyfriend?"

"Brent Johnson."

The name sounded familiar—Kim frowned.

"He's an over-the-wall guy at Fulcrum Racing."

Now she remembered. "Doesn't Wade approve?"

Sarah rolled her eyes, the same way her brother did when Kim provoked him. "He thinks Brent upsets me. Which he does, when we fight, which happens quite often. But I upset him, too, so that's okay, right?"

"I guess," Kim said doubtfully.

"Just because Wade's emotionally unavailable, that doesn't mean the rest of us can't show our feelings," Sarah huffed.

"Wade's emotionally unavailable?" Kim asked.

Sarah snorted. "He's so bossy, telling everyone what

to do, but you can never have a decent fight with him because he doesn't let anything get to him."

Kim thought about Wade's imperviousness to her insults. She'd assumed it was because he saw beyond them. It hadn't occurred to her they might bounce off him because he didn't care. She shivered.

Wade came over, tossing a tennis ball from one hand to the other as he walked—a feat of coordination Kim couldn't even begin to master. "Marco's looking for people to play catch. Want to join us?"

"I can't catch," Kim said, horrified.

"I figured that might be the case. You and I could be a double act. I'll catch, you throw."

Kim glanced at Sarah—surely a guy who didn't get involved wouldn't be so thoughtful? "I can't throw, either. You know that."

"I'll teach you," he promised.

And he did. He showed her some techniques she should have learned twenty-five years ago—how many more things were there that she should have learned but hadn't, such as how to hold the ball, how to draw her arm back properly, how to pack enough power into her throw to get the ball to go somewhere near where she wanted.

It wasn't entirely successful, but half an hour later, she was throwing with more strength and accuracy.

By the time they stopped, Kim felt more than usually tired. A glance at her watch told her she was about to be late for her dialysis...but that didn't normally make her feel nauseous. Maybe it was something she'd eaten. She sat down on the grass, rested her forehead on her knees and willed her stomach to settle.

It didn't work.

"Kim, you okay?" Wade asked.

"I think I need to get back."

He helped her to her feet. "I'll take you to Justin's motor home."

"Actually, I think I'd better get to the hotel." She had dialysate in both locations, and she had a feeling she needed a long sleep. She'd lain awake too long last night, thinking about telling Wade the truth. She'd have to do it when they got back.

The farewells to Wade's family took an age, but at last she and Wade arrived back at the hotel in a taxi. By then, Kim was sweating and shivering simultaneously.

"You're really ill," Wade said, concerned. He came around to her door, opened it and, before she could protest, scooped her into his arms.

Kim buried her face in his neck so she wouldn't have to see the stares of the people in the lobby. But apart from that minor embarrassment, this was a great place to be. Wade was warm, and he smelled of soap and sun and the outdoors. Her arms tightened around his neck.

He didn't put her down until they were inside her room. The second he released her, her knees buckled. Wade grabbed hold of her again. "I'll call a doctor."

"No. I just need to start my dialysis. I'll wash my hands, then perhaps you could help me to the bed."

He went with her to the bathroom, observed her as she went through the washing ritual that was essential to prevent her from contracting an infection through her dialysis.

Back in the bedroom, she slumped into the pillows as soon as she hit the softness of the bed. She didn't recall feeling this weak before.

Wade cursed. "What do we do now?"

"You do nothing," she said. She couldn't think of a bigger turnoff than getting involved in her dialysis.

"I'm not leaving until I'm sure you're okay," he said.

"You can bring my bag of supplies from the closet," Kim said. "Then you can wait in the bathroom while I get hooked up."

Knowing he was waiting gave her the strength to get the job done. She couldn't feel the dialysis once it started, but psychologically, she felt better right away. "You can come out now," she called.

He emerged from the bathroom looking worried. Poor guy—she'd planned to tell him about the severity of her condition; she hadn't expected to mount a graphic demonstration.

She hoped his sister was wrong about his relationships, because a raging physical attraction wouldn't be enough to keep him interested in Kim after this.

His expression cleared as he got closer. All her paraphernalia, apart from the fresh bag of dialysate hanging on a coat hook near the bed, was concealed by the bedcovers, so there was no visible cause for alarm.

"Okay," Kim said lightly. "I'm all under control, so you can go now."

ANGER AND GUILT AND shock made Wade want to hightail it out of Kim's hotel room…but at the same time chained him to her side. How the hell had she ended up so sick so fast? An hour ago, she'd been throwing a tennis ball around. Now, no matter that she was smiling, she looked so white that he was afraid she might not last the weekend.

"I'll leave in a minute," he said. With her permission, he sat on the edge of the bed, waiting for the short, panicky breaths she probably hadn't realized she was taking to lengthen and slow into a normal rhythm.

It reminded him of the hours he'd spent with his father.

He tried to think about Sunday's race, about tomorrow's practice. But even when he wasn't looking at Kim, her pale face superimposed itself on his thoughts. Dammit, she wasn't his responsibility, he didn't want to be worrying about her when he had to think about his work.

Wade realized he would have to tell Hugo about today. Kim had been on the verge of collapse. If they'd been farther away from the hotel... He stopped thinking about it.

After a few minutes, he sensed her gaze on him. She looked better than she had, her gray eyes wide open.

"I have to do the next step of my dialysis now," she said. "I'll probably fall asleep while that's happening, so you really need to leave."

Half reluctant, half eager, Wade stood.

"Thanks for your help, Wade." She wriggled against the pillows, then yawned.

"My family enjoyed meeting you today," he said, still not quite willing to walk out of there.

"They were great." She smiled at the memory. "Um, they do know you have an incredibly stressful job, right?"

"Of course," he said, puzzled.

"It's just, I noticed they demand a lot of you—a lot of support, advice. It must put pressure on you that you don't need on a race weekend."

Her perspicacity surprised him. And the fact that she was worrying about him when she was the one who was ill touched him. "That's why I don't see as much of my family as I used to. I love them all, but I had to cut back if I was ever going to get the crew chief job. It's not as if they really need me these days, I'm just a habit."

"Your sister said—" her fingers pleated the duvet "—you don't get emotionally involved with people. She seemed to be suggesting that stunts your love life."

He didn't need to ask which sister. His mouth flattened. "I don't agree with Sarah."

"So...do you get emotionally involved?"

Was it his imagination, or did she sound hopeful?

Wade's gaze in took Kim's extreme pallor, which made her face a match for the snowy pillowcase.

"I guess I will one day," he said carefully. "But right now, it's important to be single-minded about my career. It's what I want, more than anything."

There was a long silence. Then Kim said, "I'm the same—totally dedicated to my work. And busy with all this." She waved a hand over the bed.

"Uh-huh."

She looked intently at the duvet, as if studying the weave. "My dad would like me to find someone special, but—" a shaky laugh "—I guess I'm too independent. I'd never want to be a burden on a guy."

Wade knew bravado when he heard it. The right response to her declaration would have been "You could never be a burden." But she wasn't stupid, and neither was he.

When he looked back at her, her eyes were shut. *Squeezed* shut.

Wade touched her hand in sympathy, in apology. She didn't acknowledge him.

Message received.

NEXT MORNING, KIM WASN'T much better. The effort of getting herself dressed and to the racetrack brought on a rerun of last night's fatigue and nausea. When she dropped her gear in Justin's motor home, her breath was short and her ankles had swollen up—the kind of reaction she normally only had later in the day.

The smart thing would be to stay here, do her dialysis, read a book, hang out with family and hope she felt better for tomorrow's race. That's what she would do.

A desire to avoid Wade had nothing to do with it. She'd called herself all kinds of fool this morning, for imagining that he might want any kind of emotional relationship with her. He'd wanted to sleep with her, that's all.

For her to expect more was unreasonable, when right from the start he'd been the jock she planned to date and dump.

From now on, she would focus on her list. She could get a life without getting Wade Abraham.

ISABEL CHECKED THE FIGURES on the printout in front of her for the hundredth time. Whichever way she looked at it, Turn-Rite Tools received value for money from its sponsorship, and she had some suggestions that would add even more.

She'd convinced herself that Clay's tough stance on the sponsorship was a negotiating position. No one gave their final offer up front—one of the things she loved about her job was that delicate dance around the subject of money until a mutually satisfactory mating was achieved.

The primal nature of the image startled her.

Clay arrived in her office right at nine o'clock. He wasn't a tall man, but the breadth of his shoulders meant he took up an awful lot of room. He waited until she'd sat down before he did the same. Isabel had invited Dixon to be present, but although her brother had approved the numbers, he'd suggested the meeting would go better if she did it alone. He was right.

"I've prepared some numbers for you—" she slid the document across the desk "—and I'd like you to read the business case here with me, so we can discuss it right away." She didn't want to let him walk out of here and make decisions beyond the sphere of what little influence she had.

He picked up the document and began to read. Either he was a speed reader or he wasn't paying much attention, because he flipped the pages fast and it was less than five minutes before he lifted his gaze to hers. "You've done some good work."

She nodded.

He dropped the document onto the desk. "I respect you enough to lay my cards on the table."

Isabel straightened in her chair. She knew negotiating talk when she heard it. Mentally, she rehearsed Fulcrum Racing's position, and reminded herself where she would have to draw the line. "Go ahead," she invited.

"Isabel, I meant what I said about giving to the cardiac research foundation. That's my number one priority, my *only* priority. Which means Turn-Rite Tools' sponsorship of Justin Murphy will cease at the end of this season."

"What?" The rushing in Isabel's ears prevented her hearing his next words. She groped for the edge of the desk, held on, let the words wash over her. Nausea rose in her throat and she clamped her lips together.

"Isabel? Are you okay?"

She registered the question, shook her head slowly.

Clay came around the desk, used both of his hands to pry one of hers free. "You're freezing," he said roughly, chafing her fingers.

Sensation returned, and with it, pain. Dammit, she was going to cry. Isabel bit down hard on her cheeks.

Clay saw, and dropped her hand. "What the hell is going on?" he demanded. He returned to his side of the desk, and the haze in front of Isabel's eyes cleared. She examined his face and found no malice, just a hard-headed determination to do things his way. As she regained her composure, the concern in his face was replaced by a kind of perplexed irritation.

"This decision is about an incompatibility between my business needs and yours," he said. "It's not life and death."

He wouldn't understand that Fulcrum Racing *was* her life. Her family, her friends. Her past, present and future.

"If you need more for your money we can take another look at the number of sponsor appearances Justin is committed to." Her voice came out steady, a small mercy. "Or, if it's a matter of reducing the spend so that you can increase your donations to the cardiac foundation…"

"No." Clay ran a hand over his shaved head. "This isn't a negotiation, it's not empty talk. I mean every word."

CLAY DECIDED THIS WAS a good place to shut up. His less-is-more philosophy was his best hope of avoiding another outburst from Isabel. Reluctantly, he looked at her, tried to assess how she was holding up. She sounded almost her normal self, but the wounded look in her brown eyes made him feel as if he'd just kicked a puppy.

One of those yappy little dogs that never shut up, the kind he didn't like.

He'd made a business decision, one that she had to have seen coming, at least as a possibility. Dammit, sponsorship deals came and went all the time. Why should he feel guilty?

He shifted in his seat, ready to leave, but before he could stand, the office door opened. Hugo Murphy stuck his head around.

Clay hid a scowl. There was something about Murphy he just didn't like. Maybe it was that glum look permanently attached to his face.

"Excuse me, folks." Hugo nodded at Clay. "Isabel, I'm heading into meetings with Wade and Rachel, but I wanted to catch you first. I'm going to have to pull out of dinner at your place tonight, sorry."

Clay was pretty sure Isabel's day had just taken a turn for the even worse, but she drew herself up and pinned on a smile. "Oh…sure." She darted a glance at Clay, and he saw her concern for Hugo override her reluctance to have this conversation in front of him. "You don't look well. Is something wrong?"

"I'm worried about Kim." Hugo obviously saw the alarm in her face, for he said hastily, "Nothing new, it's just…it's distracting."

"Distraction" was not an okay reason to cancel a date with his girlfriend, Clay thought, disgusted.

Hugo looked uncomfortable, but he pushed on as if

he had a burden to unload. "You'd better count me out of dinner on Saturday, too."

Isabel flinched. Clay felt as if he were witnessing a death of a thousand cuts. He had unwittingly punctured some dream of hers, and now Hugo was adding a stab here, a jab there. If the guy wanted to finish with her, he should come out and say it.

He watched Isabel bring the sudden tremor of her lips under control. Her musical voice—her best feature, even if she did tend to overuse it—was slightly higher than usual when she said, "No problem."

Yeah, right. Hugo's lack of enthusiasm was clearly a big problem for her. Clay couldn't see what she saw in the guy—from what Clay had seen, he was a dour, humorless type—but coming on top of Clay's bombshell about pulling the sponsor funds, she had to be hurting.

He found he didn't like that. Which didn't make sense. Sure, Isabel was attractive—a guy'd have to be blind not to notice those curves and the great bone structure that meant she'd be beautiful into her old age. But Clay liked quiet women, women who appreciated how hard it was for him to juggle the needs of his businesses. Isabel was one-eyed about NASCAR, and she talked too much.

Right now, however, she wasn't saying a word. She looked as if she'd had too much thrown at her today, as if one more blow would topple her. Her fragility was showing.

Clay was a sucker for a fragile woman.

Hugo appeared relieved that Isabel hadn't made a fuss. Undoubtedly he'd seized the advantage of Clay's presence to pull out of Saturday's date as well as tonight's.

"So, Izzy," Clay said, and Isabel's head snapped

around to him. He'd just bet she hated being called Izzy. "Does this mean you're free for dinner on Saturday after all?"

From the corner of his eye he saw Hugo make a movement of protest. But the guy didn't have a leg to stand on. Isabel stared at Clay, and he could see that sharp mind of hers clicking over.

He helped her along. "Come on, Izzy, Hugo just took away your excuse. If you don't say yes to Saturday, I'll only keep pestering you."

Hugo's jaw dropped. Clay would have taken that as an insult, if he were Isabel, but she didn't seem to notice. She was looking at Clay, not with gratitude that he was saving her face in front of Lover-Boy, but instead with calculation.

"Dinner this Saturday?" she said slowly. "You and me?"

Now you're cottoning on, beautiful. "You'll make me a very happy man," he said. He couldn't resist a dig at Hugo: "And I don't back out of my dates."

Hugo turned a protest into a cough.

Isabel smiled widely. Damn, she was pretty. "I'd love to have dinner with you, Clay."

There was a sudden charge in the atmosphere, a shift in the balance of power that set Clay on edge.

"I'll leave you to it, then." Hugo looked as if he couldn't decide if he was relieved or resentful—he transferred his weight from one foot to the other, then back again.

You had your chance, pal.

Hugo muttered, "See you later," and left.

Isabel sank back into her chair with a stifled "oof."

"Did you mean what you said?" she asked Clay. "That you don't back out of dates?"

The urge to best Hugo was juvenile, but irresistible. "Never," Clay said.

"Good." Her expression lightened, she looked happier than she had since Clay walked in here. "Because dinner on Saturday is in California."

"Huh?"

"We'll all be at Fontana for the NASCAR Sprint Cup Series race."

"But I—" The light of challenge in her eyes had Clay biting down on his words. She'd suckered him—and not many people did that.

"Since you'll be in California, you might as well watch the race." She didn't have to say what she hoped would happen next. That he'd see the light about the sponsorship.

"Would you have gone to dinner with me here in Charlotte?" he asked. "With no race at stake?"

She didn't even hesitate before she shook her head. Clay couldn't think how he'd ever thought her fragile.

"Since I never back out of dates, I'll come to California." He pinned her with a hard glare. "But you need to know there's something else I never do."

"What's that?"

"I never back down." It was true. He'd made it to the top ahead of people better educated, richer and better bred than he was by making up his mind and sticking to it. "Don't think you'll change my mind. It's not going to happen."

CHAPTER TEN

WADE TOOK A SEAT OPPOSITE Hugo in the Fulcrum
Racing boardroom and braced himself for two unpleas-
ant but necessary tasks. One, apologize to his team-
mates for screwing up at Bristol. Two, betray Kim's
confidence and tell Hugo about her near-collapse.
Because Wade couldn't stay out of her life the way they
both needed him to unless someone else was looking
out for her.

Over the weekend, he'd justified saying nothing to
Hugo because they were busy with the race. He'd called
Kim on her cell, and she'd sounded better, had insisted
she was fully recovered. Wade wasn't about to take that
at face value, but it gave him breathing space.

Justin had finished thirty-first at Bristol, after a race
that had been a disaster from start to finish. Driver error
hadn't been the problem. Nor had the engine, nor the
efficiency of the over-the-wall crew. Nope, the problem
had been the midrace setup adjustments that Wade had
convinced Hugo to go with.

Everybody made a bad call sometimes. There wasn't
a crew chief or a car chief in NASCAR who hadn't at
one time or another screwed up a car so badly they had
to take the rap for a poor finish.

But the timing of this screwup, two weeks before the new crew chief would be appointed, couldn't be worse.

Wade had, as always, put his case for the changes to the car more forcefully than Hugo liked. Rachel had come down on Hugo's side—rightly so, as it turned out. So no matter that the Fulcrum Racing team was one of the tightest-knit, most effective teams around, when it all fell apart on Saturday, Wade had played by far the biggest part in the mess.

Now, sharing the disappointment of his colleagues around the table, he almost wondered if Hugo was right to doubt his ability to handle the crew chief job. Because a good crew chief acknowledged that people on the team had greater knowledge than he did of individual aspects of the car's setup. The shock guys knew shock absorbers inside out; the engineers had the best handle on geometry. On Saturday, Wade's determination to prove he was the best had led him to ignore the input of some of his colleagues. When Hugo had yielded to Wade's suggestions, he hadn't realized Wade was over-riding his own team's recommendations.

What at the time had seemed like instinctively brilliant decision-making looked in hindsight a lot like a bull-headed determination to prove himself. And more…deep down, Wade had known all along that his insatiable need to control every aspect of the setup was somehow linked to Kim. He'd wanted to immerse himself so fully in the car that he couldn't think about her.

It hadn't worked.

Hugo's cell phone rang, and he answered it. "Hi, Dixon."

From there, Dixon Rogers did most of the talking,

with Hugo giving occasional acknowledgment. When he ended the call, he looked unhappy. But he gave no clue as to what the conversation was about, just uncapped his pen. "Okay, folks, let's get started."

"Before we rehash Saturday's pain," Wade said, "I need to apologize to you all."

Nothing like those words to get everyone's attention—the silence was so complete, they'd have heard if someone fired up a race car a mile away.

"I don't need to tell you I messed up," Wade said, "but I want you to know I'm sorry. I'll tell the guys out there the same thing. They're the best of the best, and it wasn't right to override their skills and experience on the basis of a hunch."

"Darned right it wasn't," Hugo said, his expression inscrutable.

But both Rachel and Justin were more forgiving.

"I'm just glad it was you who screwed up this time," Rachel said, a joking reference to the engine troubles that had plagued Justin a couple of months ago.

"Yeah, and my cornering looked positively brilliant compared to the crap car you gave me," Justin added.

The mood in the room lightened, and the rest of the meeting went better than Wade thought it would. Until Hugo asked him to stay behind.

Time to tell him about Kim.

But not, it seemed, immediately.

"I appreciate you having the guts to admit you were wrong about the car," Hugo began.

Wade nodded.

"But if you ever discount the views of your team so carelessly again, you won't have a job here. Understand?"

If Wade had been the crew chief, and his car chief had done what Wade had, he'd have said the exact same thing. "Yes, sir."

He wondered if Hugo had written him off for the crew chief job. If he had, the chances Wade could turn him around before Richmond were minimal.

"Kim stayed in Justin's motor home for Saturday's race." Hugo capped his pen. "Justin said she didn't look too good. You seen her lately?"

"On Thursday."

Hugo scratched the bridge of his nose with his pen. "How'd she seem to you?"

Telling Hugo would not only free Wade of responsibility for Kim, it would help him regain some of the rapport with his boss that he'd blown out of the water during Saturday's race.

Wade hesitated. What would revealing the truth do to Kim's relationship with her father, which wasn't straightforward at the best of times? She loved Hugo a lot, and although Hugo wasn't the kind to wear his heart on his sleeve, Wade suspected he felt the same. But their interactions weren't simple.

Wade's initial determination that Hugo had every right to know about Kim's health had been diluted over the past few weeks, as his respect for Kim grew.

Until her collapse the other night had flipped Wade back in the other direction.

But if strong-minded, brave, independent Kim Murphy had her reasons for not wanting to tell Hugo how ill she was, what right did Wade have to go against her?

"The thing is, Hugo, Kim—" Dammit, he couldn't do it. "She seemed pretty tired."

Hugo grimaced. "She tires easily some days. Other days, she's got nearly as much energy as I have." He stared down at the notes he'd made during the meeting. "How're those shelves coming along?"

The abrupt change of subject confused Wade. Then he remembered Hugo had assumed he was building a set of shelves for Kim.

He was saved from having to dissemble by the arrival of Kim herself. Wearing a business suit and carrying a chocolate cake, she looked almost her normal self.

"Sorry to interrupt," she said, as she set the cake on the table. "Happy birthday, Dad."

Today was Hugo's birthday?

Hugo looked taken aback, but pleased. "Honey, shouldn't you be at work?"

"I took a couple of hours out." She turned to Wade. "Hi, Wade." Her voice was entirely casual, with no embarrassment. He revised his assessment of her appearance upward—she looked great. Her hair swung loose at her shoulders, and a light touch of makeup made her skin glow.

Wade breathed a sigh of relief—he'd done the right thing by saying nothing to Hugo. He stood. "Happy birthday, Hugo. I'll leave you two to celebrate."

Isabel came in, carrying plates and paper napkins, followed by Justin and Rachel. "Kim asked us to join you for a piece of cake," she told Hugo. She sounded defensive, Wade thought.

"Great," Hugo said, too heartily. "You stay, too, Wade." It was an order, not an invitation. In any case, Wade wasn't about to refuse an olive branch. He sat down again.

"Did you bake this?" he asked Kim.

She shook her head. "If I had, you wouldn't want to eat it. I'm a hopeless cook."

"She's the worst," Hugo agreed fondly.

Kim began passing slices of cake around. "Since I won't see you tonight, Dad, I thought I'd come in and celebrate here."

Hugo and Isabel exchanged a loaded glance.

"So, you're all set for tonight's party?" Hugo asked Kim, still sounding overly hearty.

Kim darted a glance at Wade. "Sure am." Now she was doing the hearty thing, too.

Suspicion sharpened Wade's senses. Surely she didn't have a *wild party* lined up? "What's the occasion?" he asked.

When Kim appeared not to have heard, Hugo answered. "Booth Laboratories is having a do to celebrate its silver anniversary." To Kim, he said, "Did you find a date, hon?"

Her eyes strayed to Wade. "Sure did."

Hugo brightened. "Anyone I know?"

She shook her head. "No, you don't know him."

Because he doesn't exist. Wade would bet his next pay raise that she was lying. But if she wasn't…something twisted inside Wade at the thought of Kim having a date.

Isabel finished the last morsel of her cake. "I'd better get back to work."

"Dixon called," Hugo said. "He told me the news. I'm sorry, Isabel, if I'd known when I walked in on you earlier…"

"Not a problem," she said quickly.

"What news?" Kim asked the question Wade had been about to.

Isabel sighed. "Everyone will have to know soon, but I'd rather it didn't go beyond this room just yet. Turn-Rite Tools is pulling out of Fulcrum Racing."

"You're kidding." But the grim set of Justin's mouth said he knew it was no joke.

"That's terrible." Kim sounded dismayed.

Not half as dismayed as Wade felt. Because if Turn-Rite Tools pulled out, there would be no third car for Fulcrum Racing. No crew chief job for Wade.

He cursed silently. As if she'd heard, Kim sent him a sympathetic glance. Smart as she was, she would have figured out exactly where this left him.

He cursed again as he realized something else. Not telling Hugo about Kim's collapse had put the responsibility for watching over her back in Wade's court.

What a mess.

KIM LISTENED TO PHIL Warren expounding on his views of the Charlotte real estate market—the favored topic of Booth Laboratories' staff when they were making an effort not to talk about work—with every pretense of interest.

The anniversary celebration was in full swing, in a giant tent erected in the Booth Labs parking lot. A jazz quartet played on the stage, and a few couples danced. But most people were sitting and talking, like Kim and Phil. Hopefully, it wasn't obvious that the reason she was cupping her chin in her hand was so she wouldn't fall asleep.

"If interest rates come down, I think it could be well

worth taking a plunge into the rental sector." It seemed Phil had long harbored a dream of being a landlord.

"Hmm." Kim's head spun unpleasantly. Maybe the wine was off. She blinked, and had trouble opening her eyes again. Then she wished she hadn't. Wade stood right in front of her, dressed in a tuxedo. A tall, dark Adonis.

Adonis is a myth.

Phil shook hands with Wade while Kim took an experimental swig of her wine. It didn't taste off. "Who invited you here?" She hadn't meant to sound so belligerent.

"I'm gate-crashing."

Phil looked startled.

"I'm her date," Wade reassured him. "Did you save me a dance, sweetkins?"

Sweetkins? Kim gave him the evil eye. He winked.

"I don't dance," she said. Only it came out *danshe*.

Wade gestured to her glass. "How many of those have you had?"

Kim held up two fingers. *Oops, wrong way.* She turned them around to make a peace sign. "That's all." Not that she owed him an answer.

She realized Phil had made an escape, and wondered if he'd found her as boring as she found him.

"Do you plan on having any more?"

She started to shake her head, but it made her dizzy. "No."

"Then why don't I take you home?"

"I'm waiting for this to turn into a wild party," she said.

Wade scanned the tent, the sedate couples, the clusters of quiet conversation. "I'm not sure the raw material is right."

She gave an exaggerated sigh. "Fine, we can go."

He held her chair while she stood. Kim put a hand to the table to steady herself.

"Congratulations," Wade said, "you made number four."

"Number four what?" Then she realized. "I'm not drunk," she protested.

She'd spoken way too loudly. Her boss, Jim Haynes, looked at her, a puzzled frown creasing his brow.

Wade took her hand. "Let's go, sweetkins."

The freshening wind slapped her cheeks as they crossed the road to Wade's Mustang, sobering her up. She *was* tipsy, Kim realized, and it had taken only two glasses of wine to get her that way. She was allowed to drink alcohol as long as she stayed within her fluid restrictions, but she seldom bothered.

By the time they reached her condo she'd steadied up a lot.

Wade saw her inside. "Need any help getting your dialysis going?"

"I'll be fine," she said, enunciating clearly now. He searched her face, then nodded.

Kim put down her purse on the console in the hallway. "Did you come tonight so you could rescue me?"

He shook his head. "I didn't expect to find you drunk."

She decided not to debate the exact level of her inebriation. "I told you I had a date. You didn't believe me, did you?"

He spread his hands in apology. "You're not very good at asking guys out on dates."

"Good point." She headed for the kitchen and Wade followed. "Coffee?" She could probably only drink a quarter of a cup before she reached her fluid limit, but it was worth the effort even for that small dose of caffeine.

"Sure."

While they waited for the kettle to boil, they talked about the Turn-Rite Tools disaster. Kim was thankful to have this chance to have an ordinary conversation with him, one that didn't involve her health or his lack of interest in a relationship. The buffer of her alcohol intake helped, leaving her dazed enough not to recall all the details of that humiliating evening in Bristol, and loosening her tongue. By the time he left tonight, they should be able to greet each other as the friends she'd told him she wanted to be. He must want the same, or he wouldn't be here.

Kim poured the coffee and passed a mug to Wade. She remembered the first time she'd had coffee with him, how nervous she'd been.

"You know what I like about you?" she said.

"My ability to make you feel intellectually inferior?"

She giggled—nope, she wasn't sober yet. "You give me confidence. I'm not sure how, but you do."

He sipped his coffee, then put the mug on the counter. "Kim, you're confident because you have every reason to be. It's nothing to do with me." She protested, and he said, "So what if you can't make small talk? Look at Isabel, she's a fount of conversational trivia and it hasn't made her happy."

"I never thought of that." Kim blew on her coffee to cool it. "Not that I'd call Isabel's conversation trivia."

"Whereas you," he said, "can make oncogenes sound sexy."

"I can't," she said, startled.

"I love it when you use those big words."

"Really?" Kim thought he was teasing, but the light in his eyes suggested there was at least a hint of truth in his words.

"Really," he said. "Come on, sweetkins, talk smart to me."

Kim started to laugh.

"I mean it," Wade protested. "Say something smart, just for me." He sounded utterly serious.

Kim put down her mug. "Okay," she said slowly. "How's this? There's some evidence that scientists might be able to reverse differentiation in mice cells, allowing adult cells to become pluripotent."

Wade grasped her hands. "You're incredible, what a gal." His thumbs caressed her palms. "Say it again, sweetkins."

Laughing, she did. Wade pulled her into his arms. "Not fair," he said softly. "You're tormenting me."

"And I thought *I* was pathetic," she said.

Wade kissed her, deeply, languorously. She knew it was just a kiss, that there would be no more than that, but she wanted it, so she took it.

ISABEL WIPED OFF THE crimson lipstick she'd applied and replaced it with a more neutral, brownish tone, before she inspected herself in the hotel room's full-length mirror. But the new shade on her lips made her green dress look muddy. She wiped her mouth with a tissue, then went back to her original choice.

A knock on the door startled her. She wafted a quick blast of hairspray over her hair—control was the order of the night—and went to open it.

"Hugo." What awful timing.

Hugo said awkwardly, "I wanted to catch you before you go out on your date."

"It's not a date." She hurried to reassure him. "It was just a way to get Clay here to California."

But Hugo wasn't listening. He spread his fingers at his sides. "I came to say that, if you do want to date Mortimer, you should go ahead."

Isabel blinked. "Excuse me?"

He ran a hand around the back of his neck, didn't meet her eyes. "Isabel, I like you a lot. I'd hoped you and I could make a go of things long-term. But…I don't think we should continue seeing each other."

Two thoughts hit her simultaneously: one, he was dumping her; and two, they were having this awful conversation practically in the hotel corridor. She stepped backward, almost stumbled, and he followed her into the room.

She used the time it took to click the door carefully shut to take three deep breaths. Her insides still churned, but she calmly managed to ask, "Is there a problem?"

"No…yes." Hugo closed his eyes, and when he opened them, she was shocked at the raw pain there. "Isabel, I'm trying to find Sylvie."

Isabel swallowed. She'd always suspected Hugh held a tender spot for the stupid, cruel woman who'd left him. "It's been nearly thirty years. You can't still love her."

He recoiled. "Of course I don't love her. But she might be a donor match for Kim. She's the best chance we have." He paced to the mirror, ignored the clutter of cosmetics and hair products Isabel had used in her careful attempt to look good without giving Clay the impression she was available.

"Thinking about Sylvie and Kim's illness made me realize I'm not ready for a serious relationship right now. I need to give Kim my full attention," Hugo said. "You're too smart, too beautiful to settle for less than a man who'll give you his all. I don't want you to think that one day I might be that man."

That old line—*I'm doing this for your sake, not mine.* Scalding tears pricked at Isabel's eyes. She wanted to slap Hugo's face and call him a fool who would never find a woman better for him than she was.

"I understand," she lied. "I appreciate your honesty." She cursed her inescapable good manners. Hugo was dumping her, and she was practically saying thank you. She let him kiss her cheek—if she'd had any spunk she'd have turned her head and bitten his nose!

By THE TIME SHE WALKED into the downtown Fontana restaurant where she'd agreed to meet Clay, Isabel had overshot self-loathing and landed firmly in fury. All she'd ever wanted was to preserve the NASCAR-centered existence that was her source of happiness, and now, two men were set to ruin everything.

Hugo and Clay.

One had destroyed her vision of a shared future; the other was determined to put Fulcrum Racing through hell.

She spotted Clay across the restaurant—he saw her in the same moment and rose from his chair. His punctuality and his courtesy didn't abate her fury one iota. The man might be enormously successful, but he couldn't add two and two together to see that Turn-Rite Tools' increased public profile was directly linked to its NASCAR sponsorship.

"Hello, Isabel." He stood as she approached.

"Clay," she snarled, and his eyebrows lifted.

His gaze roved her green velvet dress, cut low in front and slim-fitting at her waist and hips. "You look good."

He kept looking, couldn't seem to take his eyes off her, and she gathered that "good" was Clay's idea of a compliment.

She sat down and buried her face in the menu while she regrouped her thoughts. She'd insisted Clay come to California because she wanted another chance to convince him to keep the Turn-Rite sponsorship. She assumed he'd offered the date out of some competitive male thing he had going with Hugo, whom it was obvious Clay didn't like. But now it seemed he was attracted to her. She would be foolish to squander that attraction.

Her mom used to say you catch more flies with honey than vinegar.

The waiter poured them each a glass of the Napa sauvignon blanc Clay had ordered. As Isabel tasted it, she consciously discarded her bad mood, and pulled on her social façade.

She chatted about the preparations for tomorrow's race, for which Justin had qualified in sixth position. She said too much, of course, and she could see that Clay was waiting for her to stop talking. Waiting patiently, this time.

"I've been doing some reading," he said when she let him get a word in, "about Fulcrum Racing."

He was taking an interest in the team? This had to be good. "You'll have seen that we have a rich NASCAR tradition," she said.

He nodded. "Back in, what, ninety-five, the team

finished first, second and third in the championship series?"

She could remember that moment as if it were yesterday. Standing in the pits at the Homestead track with her parents, with Dixon, screaming her elation as the three Fulcrum Racing cars, back then sporting a red, white and blue color scheme, had taken the checkered flag in quick succession, and with it, the top three slots in the championship series.

"It was glorious." Her voice shook. "Simply glorious."

He sat back, studied her. "And then your parents died, just a few weeks later."

She nodded, mute. She still couldn't think of her parents' tragic end without a shock wave rippling through her. "They were on vacation—they hardly ever took one, but they deserved it after such a phenomenal season," she said. "They were in Australia. A sudden storm hit while they were playing golf, and they took shelter under a tree." The stupidity of it still stunned her. The most basic mistake had killed her parents.

"I read that lightning struck the tree and electrocuted them both," Clay said quietly.

Isabel blinked, and was grateful to have the time the waiter spent setting her mixed seafood starter down to regain her composure. She picked up her fork, studied her plate as if the choice whether to start with a prawn or a steamed clam was all-important. "Mom was killed instantly. Dad was badly burned and died a few days later."

Clay said nothing for so long, she was forced to look at him. "I'm sorry," he said.

She nodded, forked a clam out of its shell and into her mouth.

"So you and Dixon took over the team." He started in on his onion soup.

She forced herself to tell him, for the sake of the team, for the sake of the money Clay controlled.

"Dixon inherited sixty percent of Fulcrum Racing. I got the family home and the condo at the racetrack in Charlotte, along with the remaining forty percent of the team.

"If Mom and Dad had lived, everything would have been fine. But neither Dixon nor I was ready to step up to the plate, though we should have been. We made mistakes, mainly in our choice of personnel. Then Dixon accused another team of cheating—he can get pretty hotheaded about fair play," she said, proud of her brother despite the price they'd paid for his impetuosity, "and they sued us. It distracted us from our racing and cost a lot of money.

"For a long time, we dropped down to just one cup car. A couple of years ago we got the second car going— that was a huge milestone. Next year, we plan to run three cars."

And when that happened, Fulcrum Racing would have found its way back to glory days. The Rogers name would once again be spoken with reverence in the same breath as the names of NASCAR's founders, rather than being a byword for all that could go wrong when teams didn't manage their succession planning.

"Getting back on track has cost you and your brother a lot." Clay's blue eyes were shrewd.

"We've put everything into it," Isabel admitted. "Both of us. Both our marriages broke up."

Clay let out a whistling breath between his teeth. "Do you have kids?"

She swallowed the old grief and said steadily, "I was pregnant when my parents were killed, and I lost the baby soon after. Brad—my husband—thought we were too old to try again, and I was so busy with the team I didn't argue." How she'd cursed herself for that too-easy capitulation! "A couple of years later we split up, so I guess it was for the best."

Isabel lifted her wineglass, closed her eyes on the pretense of inhaling the delicate, grassy bouquet. Telling Clay these things only served to remind her that she couldn't let him pull out of his sponsorship without doing everything she could to change his mind.

Even if she had to beg.

What did the Rogers pride matter when they were a laughingstock among the people whose respect they'd once commanded? When Isabel's happiness—and Dixon's—would remain tantalizingly beyond their reach until they restored the team to its rightful place?

She put down her glass, put every scrap of entreaty into her eyes, her voice. "Clay, you told me you never back down, but I'm asking you—I'm *begging* you—to reconsider your decision."

When he didn't say the immediate, decisive "no" she expected, hope burgeoned. "I know the cardiac research is important to you, and it's a worthy cause, but—"

"Actually, you *don't* know." Clay pushed his soup bowl away. "Isabel, I've given this a lot of thought. But it wouldn't matter how good your business case is, I made a commitment ten years ago that I'm not prepared to back out of."

Isabel tried to dissect his words to find a thread of hope. She failed. "What commitment?" she probed.

He hesitated. "The cardiac research foundation is called the Elizabeth Mortimer Foundation."

She knew then. "Your wife?"

He nodded. "Beth died ten years ago. Every spare dollar I earn goes to help make sure other people don't suffer the way she did."

How was Isabel supposed to argue with that? How could she even *want* to, how could she compare her family's pride with this man's memorial to his beloved wife?

"I didn't realize. I'm sorry." She groped for a path that would find a way through the conversation without letting Fulcrum Racing's hopes die. "Were you married long?"

"Thirteen years. Beth had a bad heart from the beginning. We always knew we weren't likely to see out our old age together, always knew we wouldn't have kids."

"You must have treasured the years you had." Whereas Isabel and Brad had squandered the years of their marriage on petty squabbles.

FOR ONE MOMENT, Clay was transported back to the days of his marriage. Those years had gone fast, time passing almost without him noticing. But then, he'd been busy. He toyed with his steak knife. "I spent a lot of time traveling."

Isabel frowned. "While your wife was ill?"

Clay heard disapproval in the question. He *had* treasured the time he and Beth had together, though maybe not in the way other people did. Still, he found himself getting defensive.

"Beth's health wasn't too bad the first five years of

our marriage. When she got worse I cut back on the travel. But we weren't used to spending time together— we drove each other nuts." He shook his head at the memory. Even though by then he could afford a large home, it hadn't been big enough for the two of them. "Beth insisted I go back to my normal routine."

He hadn't put up much of a fight. He'd loved Beth for the things that made her different from him—her gentleness, her quietness, the frailty that called to his protective instincts. Their marriage had never been a true partnership.

"She sounds like a brave woman." Isabel's comment sounded not so much a commendation of Beth as a criticism of Clay.

"She wasn't a martyr, if that's what you mean," Clay growled. "Beth didn't like being ill, but she loved that I could live large enough for the two of us."

He knew how it looked—as if he'd done whatever he wanted, then come home and rubbed his wife's nose in the fact that he was healthy and she wasn't. But it hadn't been like that at all. "I always put her first," he said.

Isabel's face cleared, and he thought she understood. Then her cutlery thudded onto the table, clattering against her plate. "Garbage," she said, loud enough for people nearby to turn and stare.

Clay felt his face redden. "What the hell does that mean?"

Her hands fisted on the table. "I'm so sick of men who delude themselves they think of anyone other than themselves. You did what suited you. Beth's needs didn't come into it."

"You know nothing about it," he snapped. "I loved my wife."

"Husband of the year," she mocked, and Clay's eyes glazed with anger so that she became an accusing green blur in front of him. "Or maybe you're runner-up to Brad, my ex, who was kind enough to leave me because he—" she made quote marks with her fingers "—'could never be the man to make me happy.' And in third place comes Hugo. Of course, he'll never be my husband, now that he dumped me as a *favor* to me."

"He dumped you?" The news jerked Clay out of his righteous anger, set an odd excitement churning in his gut. That explained Isabel's oversensitivity. But he couldn't feel too sorry for her. Anyone could see Hugo wasn't right for her.

She ignored him. "You can delude yourself you were a good husband, Clay, but from where I'm sitting, you were too selfish to be the man your wife needed. Instead, your guilty conscience has you throwing money at her memory."

Now that he knew where she was coming from, her words didn't even sting. This wasn't about him and Beth, it was about Hugo and Isabel. "You have every right to be bitter, sweetheart, but you'll get over Crew Chief Guy."

The "sweetheart" had just slipped out, and Clay was shocked to realize he wanted to take her in his arms and comfort her. Maybe not right now—she looked mad enough to do some damage to a man's sensitive parts with her dinner knife—but soon.

"You don't get to talk to me about Hugo," she said.

"And you don't get to call me 'sweetheart.' I need an emotionally mature man in my life, and I need a sponsor for Justin. You're out on all counts."

And with that, Isabel Rogers, the woman who talked too much, who cared too much about another man, whose only interest in Clay was the money he could offer her team—and who had just become the first woman Clay had wanted to sleep with in ten years—pushed back her chair, abandoned her unfinished meal and stalked out of the restaurant.

THE BUILDUP TO THE NASCAR Sprint Cup Series race at Fontana was stressful enough without Wade having to broker a peace deal between his sister and her adolescent boyfriend.

"No, I will not ask Brent if he still loves you," he told Sarah, exasperated. "Ask him yourself. *After* the race."

Brent wasn't really adolescent, of course. He just acted that way, and Sarah was even worse. The young couple had been dating on and off—mostly off—for a year. They had the most volatile relationship Wade had ever seen, even by his family's standards. As Wade saw it, Sarah, who as the youngest in the family had ended up somewhat spoiled—though still entirely lovable—gave Brent hell.

The guy was dumb enough to take it, but every so often he'd snap. World War Three would blow up, and their big romance was all over. Until next week, when a tearful reconciliation—Wade had actually seen Brent crying, poor sap—would restore love's young dream.

"I can't ask him myself." Sarah craned her head to see Brent hanging out with the other over-the-wall crew in the pits while they waited for the prerace ceremony to begin. "He's looking," she hissed.

Wade rolled his eyes. "I'll tell him to concentrate on his job." He couldn't understand why Sarah put herself through this.

"Don't, he's upset. I can see it in his eyes."

Given the guy was fifty feet away, his sister must have incredible powers of vision.

"If you got to know him a little better, you'd see why I love him," Sarah said.

Wade seriously doubted that. "I work with him. I know him."

"You work on the car, Brent does the gas. You've barely exchanged a dozen words."

It was true. As long as Brent kept down the time it took him to top off the No. 448 car's fuel cell, Wade had no interest in him. And Brent, for all his emotional weaknesses, was fast. "I do know that for every good day you guys have, you have one where you're in tears. It's not healthy."

"It's not *healthy* to be so scared to take a risk that you—"

"Give it a rest, Sarah." Wade glanced around at the crowded pits. Wasn't it time they started the national anthem?

"What do you think, Kim?" Sarah raised her voice to attract Kim's attention.

Kim excused herself from Isabel, to whom she'd been chatting next to the pit box, and joined them. "What do I think about what?"

"People can't be happy if they're so scared of getting hurt they never take a risk, can they?"

Wade wasn't thrilled that Sarah had dragged Kim into their conversation, but he was confident that, despite that little glitch in Bristol, Kim's independence and her logical approach to life meant she would see things differently. Hopefully, she would shut his little sister up.

Kim said, "I've always thought it's wiser not to let yourself get hurt."

Ha!

"But," she added, "lately I've been wondering if I'm missing out. If I want more ups in my life, maybe I need to risk having more downs."

"See?" Sarah turned triumphantly to Wade. "Thanks, Kim. I'm going to see Brent right now and tell him I love him." Sarah marched off toward the hapless Brent.

"You don't take risks," Wade said to Kim.

"I didn't used to," she agreed. "I've changed."

He folded his arms. "You're not talking about your list, are you?"

"That…and other things."

Wade had a sneaking suspicion she was talking about her relationship with him. Which, dammit, wasn't risky, because he didn't plan on getting emotionally involved, and she'd better not, either.

"If you want to take a risk," he said, "why don't you tell your father how sick you got at Bristol? Why don't you ask him outright if he'll ever stop loving you, rather than tread carefully around him just in case?"

Her sharp intake of breath told Wade he'd hurt her.

Yeah, well, too bad. If Kim wanted to take emotional risks in her life, she didn't get to do it with him. He didn't want to lurch from one crisis to another like

Sarah. He didn't want to be consumed with worry about someone he loved.

Someone had to take a reality check around here, and Wade wasn't afraid to do it.

CHAPTER ELEVEN

ON LAP EIGHTY-SIX, Justin's left rear tire exploded. Hugo cursed as smoke filled the monitor screen, and Justin came on the radio to report what he thought had happened.

He had no choice but to limp to the pits. Wade had his team ready to check out the damage, but no one held out much hope that the No. 448 car could finish anywhere near the front.

But when the crew got into the wheel well, they discovered minimal damage—no rubber wrapped around the axle, and the brake line was almost a hundred percent intact. They could work with this.

Wade's crew got a new tire on the car right away, and Wade made the call to send Justin back out so he wouldn't lose too many places. They would fix the small amount of damage to the brake line at the next pit stop. A lucky caution meant that wasn't too far away, and by lap one hundred, the car was back to full performance.

When Justin roared past them on the frontstretch, passing two cars as he did so, the cheer that went up from the Fulcrum Racing pits was almost as deafening as the car.

ISABEL HADN'T EXPECTED TO SEE Clay at the race, so she was annoyed at how keenly she felt his absence when the green flag fell and the cars surged over the line. It must be because all hope of preserving the Turn-Rite Tools sponsorship had gone.

How could Fulcrum Racing hope to compete with the Elizabeth Mortimer Foundation? And even if it could…she'd been so upset about Hugo that she'd been unpardonably rude to Clay. For all she knew, he and his wife had been perfectly happy in their unusual situation.

Two-thirds of the way into the race, Clay arrived in the sponsor suite. Isabel's heart lurched, a reaction so unexpected that she wondered if she should book in for a physical.

As she went to greet him, she noticed a couple of the other women in the suite turn to look at him. For the first time, she realized he was attractive. She'd noticed his mouth before, but now she could see that the whole Clay Mortimer package could be distinctly appealing, if a woman liked that overt, assertive masculinity, that weathered face. Going by the way those women were eyeing him, they liked it a lot. Irritation prickled through Isabel. They could be more subtle—the man was a widower, still smitten with his late wife. She found herself consciously blocking their view as she walked toward Clay.

"Isabel." His smile was unexpectedly warm, and Isabel blushed.

"I'm sorry for what I said last night." She rushed the words before she lost her nerve. "I had no right."

Was it her imagination, or was he standing unusually close to her? No, not her imagination, because she could see the new growth of whiskers just beneath the skin of his jaw.

"I deserved it," he said. "I gave you some bad news, on top of…other bad news."

His fingers brushed against hers, a casual gesture of sympathy, but it set Isabel's hand tingling. Silence rose between them, and though she tried to resist, she had to fill it. "It looks like we're in for a great race today. Did you see how well Justin was doing right before he pitted? He got past Bart Branch and held him off for ten laps. If he hadn't had to come in, he'd have made it past Cruise as well."

"I saw." Impulsively, he said, "Watch the race with me, Izzy. Someone needs to tell me why the No. 414 car didn't pit when everyone else did."

She was too pleased that he'd forgiven her outburst last night to call him on the *Izzy*. "That's Dean Grosso." She craned to see Dean heading into Turn One. "He's a lap behind since he got tangled up with Trent Matheson earlier. His crew chief will be hoping he can pit under caution soon."

She watched most of the race with Clay—and found she enjoyed his company more than she had when she'd been hounding him about the sponsorship. It was a pleasant change not to have to read every word Clay said for a clue as to her fate.

Justin finished eighteenth after a few late-race car problems. Hugo would be disappointed, Isabel thought. Then tried to unthink it.

Some of Turn-Rite's clients stayed on drinking long after the team would have packed up the car and left. So Isabel was startled when Hugo strolled by nearly two hours after the checkered flag fell, just as the last guests, except Clay, were leaving.

She'd been so angry with Hugo last night, she hadn't expected the stab of hurt. Involuntarily, she pressed a hand to her chest.

"You okay?" Clay was right beside her, looking where she was looking—at Hugo talking to Dixon.

"I, uh, guess Dixon must have offered Hugo a ride on our plane." She bit her lip, unsure if she was ready to face him.

Clay's hand landed on her arm, heavy and warm. "You can fly back with me, if you like."

Some of his fighting spirit seemed to seep into her. Isabel shook her head. "Thanks, but I might as well get it over with."

He nodded. "Good girl."

"I'm fifty years old." She felt compelled to make it clear she was no longer a girl.

"Just a young thing," he said. "I'm fifty-eight."

For a second, the admiration in his eyes did make her feel young.

"Isabel," Dixon called. "I'm going with Hugo to get some papers from his motor home. Do you want to call a cab for the airport and meet us out front in fifteen minutes?"

"Sure," she told him, relieved that she'd been smiling when Hugo had looked at her. The two men left—only Isabel and Clay remained, along with a couple of staff tidying up.

Isabel felt suddenly awkward. "I'd better call that cab."

"Uh-huh."

"Is this—" she cleared her throat "—the last race

you'll come to? I know you're not a particular fan, and now that you've made the decision to can the sponsorship…" The prospect of never seeing him again left her feeling strangely hollow.

"Not a particular fan," he mused. "I'm not so sure about that."

"*Are* you a fan?" she asked, surprised.

"A fan of what?"

The gleam in his eyes disconcerted her. "Of… NASCAR," she said, suddenly short of breath.

"I'm a fan of something."

Before she could even guess his intention, he leaned in, kissed her on the mouth.

And not a quick peck, either, Isabel registered even as something—*good manners!*—had her returning the kiss. Clay's mouth was hard and demanding, just like the man, yet there was something strangely seductive about that no-frills, no-quarter-asked-or-given kiss. Her eyelids fluttered closed, heightening the sensation. But when he increased the pressure, demanding entry, she balked. She twisted her head away, shocked at how much effort that simple movement required.

He was breathing heavily, and for a long moment, he regarded her through hooded eyes. Then he said abruptly, "Good night, Izzy."

And left Isabel swaying on her feet. Unsettled in a way she hadn't been since…well, since last time she saw Clay.

CLAY STRODE INTO ISABEL'S office at nine o'clock on Monday morning, which showed how little he knew, she thought with exasperation. Normally she wouldn't be here at this time on a Monday—like most of the team, she made a late start the day after a race. But she hadn't slept well last night, and if she wasn't sleeping, she might as well be at the office.

She'd already decided that if she had to see Clay again to wrap up the sponsorship contract, they were going to pretend that kiss hadn't happened. She donned her best sponsor liaison expression. "Good morning."

"Not yet." He closed the door behind him.

"Excuse me?"

He advanced purposefully and, to her alarm, didn't stop when he reached her desk. He came around it, until he was right in front of her, making her lean back to see his face.

"So far it's been a damned awful morning," he said.

"Oh." Hardly her most inspired comment.

"I couldn't sleep last night for thinking about that kiss." His eyes burned like blue flames, their heat licking at Isabel.

So much for not talking about it. Clay grabbed her hands, and she gasped as he tugged her out of her chair.

"Admit it," he demanded. "You've been thinking about it, too. I can see it in those circles under your eyes."

She should be offended at that ungentlemanly observation, yet all she felt was excitement. She moistened her lips with her tongue, saw his eyes narrow in interest. "It crossed my mind," she admitted. "Once or twice."

Clay didn't need more. His laugh was exultant, as he wrapped his arms around her for a repeat performance.

Only this kiss was far more powerful.

Maybe yesterday's warm-up, unsettling as it had been, had given them a degree of familiarity. Isabel parted her lips immediately, willingly, beneath his, unbecomingly eager for his exploration. She might have known Clay would kiss like a race car driver facing a green flag. Foot to the floor, no holds barred in an attempt to gain an early advantage.

She yielded without a fight, too intent on sampling this strange new caress. Then, gradually, an unfamiliar instinct took over, telling her to stake her claim every bit as thoroughly as he staked his. She shifted in his embrace, pressed her curves to him. Clay groaned, an intoxicating sound, and his hands moved down over her hips, her derriere.

Isabel let her own hands wander somewhere she only now realized they'd been longing to go. Around Clay's neck, and up over that intriguing, exciting, shaved head. Caressing that soft, smooth skin over hard bone was one of the most sensual things she'd experienced, and she had the craziest urge to ask him to make love to her.

She hauled her errant senses back into line, broke off the kiss and stepped away from him, palms pressed to her hot cheeks.

"*Now* it's a good morning." Clay's voice was rough with satisfaction.

Isabel sank into her chair. "I didn't expect to see you again so soon," she said. "Maybe not ever."

He barked a laugh. "No hope of that now, beautiful."

"Clay…" She picked up a pen, put it down again. "That was a mistake."

"That's not how it felt."

No, indeed. She shook her head to clear the confusion. "I just broke up with Hugo," she said. "I can only think that kissing you was a rebound thing."

Instead of taking offence, he laughed. Isabel realized

she liked his laugh. It was warm but slightly hoarse, as if he'd once been a smoker.

"If you think the connection between us is some kind of leftover from your fling with Murphy—" he walked around to the other side of the desk and planted his hands so he was looking directly at her "—you couldn't be more wrong. It's ten years—more than that—since a woman had me this hot and bothered. I want to go on seeing you."

For one second, she was tempted. Then logic prevailed. "Even if I wasn't on the rebound…you're an attractive man, but you're not the kind of man I date."

"Let me guess," he said, "you date guys with engine oil running through their veins. Men who can trace their motor-racing ancestry back to the invention of the wheel."

"Yes," she said. Because although she'd allowed herself to be carried away by the mastery of Clay's mouth, his hands, he was right. Isabel stood. "You and I…it's not what I want. Not for more than a few seconds."

CLAY'S MIND RACED, egged on by frustration. Dammit, he'd just figured out he wanted Izzy, and he wasn't about to take no for an answer.

But she wasn't like Beth, she wasn't… His mind shied away from the word *aimless* on the grounds of potential disloyalty. Isabel wasn't *biddable,* that was it— she was too committed to her own goals to yield to his.

But Clay always got what he wanted. And he knew that sometimes, you had to give the other guy what he wanted first.

He flung himself into the chair opposite the desk— *I'm not going anywhere*—and leaned forward. "What if," he said to Isabel, "there was a way I could keep Turn-Rite's sponsorship going?"

After a moment's incomprehension, her face lit up in a way it hadn't when Clay had said he'd like to keep seeing her.

"Really?"

"Not at the expense of the cardiac research," he said gruffly. "But there might be a way to make the pie bigger. Maybe I can get costs down in one of my other businesses, and leave Turn-Rite alone for a while." All his companies ran leanly, but if he told his financial people to make it happen…

Isabel pushed her chair back from her desk. "Are you saying there's a link between your willingness to sponsor Justin and my willingness to date you?"

"I'm saying I'll spend the next few weeks making a genuine effort to make the sponsorship work," he said. "And in that time, I would like the pleasure of your company. Three weeks should be enough."

He meant three weeks should be enough for him to get Izzy out of his system. He grinned at the thought that by then she'd have talked his ears off. He didn't see himself marrying a woman like her—didn't see himself ever marrying again. But for now, for a few weeks, he had to have her.

"That takes us through to Dover," she said. "And after that?"

He shrugged. "If we can make the sponsorship work, it'll go ahead. If we can't, you'll know I did my damnedest. Whether you and I keep seeing each other is entirely separate."

She nodded. "That sounds…an acceptable way of

dealing with our attraction. But, Clay, I won't necessarily…"

"I won't ask you to do anything you don't want to." Clay was confident of his powers of persuasion.

"Then—" she drew a sharp breath "—we have a deal." She looked suddenly nervous, as she stuck out her hand.

Clay took it, drew it to his mouth, kissed her knuckles. Then nipped.

"Oh!" Isabel's eyes widened, but she didn't pull away. Clay kissed each knuckle in turn.

"Dinner tomorrow night," he ordered. "I'll pick you up at seven."

As he took down her address, he shut out the thought that he'd just committed to spend tens of thousands of dollars investigating the feasibility of a NASCAR sponsorship that could end up costing him millions more—all so he could date Isabel Rogers for three weeks.

When he walked out of her office, he left behind the battered, bruised remains of his ego and his sanity— twin victims of his infatuation with Isabel Rogers.

AT HOME ON MONDAY NIGHT, Wade struggled to concentrate on the California race he'd recorded. It wasn't the first time that had happened lately.

On one occasion after another, he found himself thinking about Kim when he should have been thinking about his work. He'd be mentally replaying a race, accurately recalling every move of Justin's car on the track, when he'd remember one of her sassy comments about jock mating rituals. Or some debate they'd had about race strategy or stem cell ethics. He loved pitting his wits against hers, never knowing which of them was going to come out on top in a particular encounter.

Then there were the times when he caught himself worrying about her health. If she didn't show up at practice, if she looked pale, if she picked at her food.

His preoccupation with Kim was a distraction Wade couldn't afford. And he especially couldn't afford to worry about her health. Next thing, he'd be ducking out of races to look after her, and what the hell would that do for his hopes of becoming a crew chief? Especially given the new rumor that Turn-Rite was reconsidering its plans to drop the sponsorship.

Wade needed to wrap up this whatever-it-was he had going with Kim, and get back into the groove.

He hit the remote to turn off the TV. The key to it all was Kim's list. The list was where this had started. It made sense that finishing the list should finish the relationship.

Mentally, he ran through those teenage goals of hers. She'd played hooky, dated a jock, got the wimpiest tattoo the world had ever seen, bought a push-up bra... His mind wandered for a moment. And she'd gotten drunk—he wondered if any other woman was as cute as Kim when she was drunk.

She still had to make out at the movies, be the life and soul of a wild party and drive a stock car. And dump a jock.

All Wade had to do was make those things happen—soon.

Making out at the movies seemed too intimate, given Wade's current tendency to distraction. He'd save that for some time when he had his full defenses in place. But the wild party...there was plenty of partying in

NASCAR. Wade had been known to be the life and soul of one or two shindigs himself.

His imagination balked at the vision of Kim doing the same. But she was one determined lady, so maybe she could.

He picked up the phone and called a couple of party animals he knew. Ten minutes later, he had an invitation to a party on Thursday night in Richmond. He knew Kim planned to take a vacation day on Friday, so she could be at the track Thursday evening.

Now he had to make sure she was the life and soul of the bash. He wasn't about to risk her failing, because then he'd have to find another party, and that would prolong this thing. Wade picked up his phone again.

KIM PAUSED IN THE doorway of the Jezebel nightclub, venue for her first-ever wild party.

"Scared?" Wade said into her ear.

She shook her head and said loud enough to be heard over the music, "Just working out where to start being the life and soul of this thing."

She was also trying to figure out if the outfit she'd chosen fit in okay. Nothing in her wardrobe had qualified as a life-and-soul-of-a-party outfit. She'd had to buy a new ensemble.

She'd chosen a short dark skirt whose side slit might just give people a glimpse of her tattoo, and a slinky, silver halter top that required her to go braless, but whose clever draping still managed to make her look relatively shapely.

She'd also applied more makeup than usual, using color to emphasize her eyes and the fullness of her lips, the way Isabel had showed her.

Wade grabbed her hand. "You look gorgeous. Quit thinking, Dr. Brains, and jump on in."

He pulled her into the crowd before Kim could even think *I'm not ready.* Almost immediately, they found a couple of guys from Fulcrum Racing. Their presence made her more comfortable, even though their manner toward her was slightly reserved, as if she might go blabbing to her father tomorrow about whatever they got up to tonight. Or as if they thought she was boring.

Then they were joined by another man, one Wade apparently knew. "Kim, this is Andy," he said.

Andy's eyes lit up. "Hey, babe."

I'm a babe? "Hey," she said. *Hey* sounded so much cooler than *hi,* she should use it more often.

"How about a dance?" Andy said.

Uh-uh. There was no one on the dance floor yet, and Kim didn't plan to be first.

Then Wade murmured, close to her ear, "This is your chance," and gave her a little shove. Before she knew what was happening, she and Andy had stepped off the carpet and onto the scuffed wooden dance floor.

If Kim had ever thought about it, she'd have said she wasn't confident of her abilities as a dancer. Or at least, of her ability to look cool while dancing. Which meant coming to a party like this was a rash move.

Andy began to move in a free-form, gangly kind of dance. She tried to emulate him. But it evidently involved loosening one's shoulders almost to the point of dislocation…and she was way too uptight.

She was hardly moving and she looked like a nerd, Kim thought, panicking. She sent a beseeching look to

Wade. He gave her a grin and a nod that said he had every confidence in her.

Stupid, dumb jock.

She'd have to try a more structured approach, Kim decided. Maybe it was that she was standing on a dance floor for the first time in years, but suddenly, memories of the ballroom dancing classes she'd attended in high school—when Hugo insisted she take up some kind of sport and she couldn't stand to do anything else—surfaced.

Ballroom dancing in a nightclub? Andy didn't look as if he could waltz. Besides, the beat of the music was much too fast. The only traditional dance she could imagine fitting into this rhythm was the Charleston.

Could she Charleston at a wild party?

Tentatively, Kim stretched her arms in front of her, then bent her elbows up with her fingers straight and her palms out. She moved them in the windscreen-wiper-style motion that was an essential part of the Twenties dance.

Andy didn't freak out, which she took as a good sign. She sped up the movement, and gave a couple of experimental little kick-steps. Her partner's eyebrows went up, but so did his thumbs.

What the heck. Either I come out of this looking so stupid that I can set up a new career as a party clown, or I'll have people asking me for dance lessons. She launched into a full-on Charleston: stepped back with her right foot, kicked back with her left, then forward with her left foot, kicked forward with her right. Then she repeated the process, keeping her arms going, too.

It felt great to move with such energy. She'd be exhausted later, but she didn't care. She became aware of people drifting toward the dance floor. A couple of others joined them, but most were just observing. Kim felt her cheeks heating, not entirely from the exertion. Concentrating hard on her moves, she only noticed just in time that the song had ended, and she came to a sudden stop.

Breathing heavily, she eyed her partner.

"Cool moves," he said. Which said more about his youth than it did about her skill.

"Thanks," she panted. The next song started, and it was just as lively as the last one. Kim found her partner's place taken by another man she'd never met, one who seemed to move considerably faster than the last guy and was evidently expecting her to repeat her performance. It would look odd if she went through the same routine again—and besides, this song was a little slower. She managed to combine some Charleston moves with some judicious swaying, which didn't exhaust her quite as much.

Several dances later, she was still on the floor when Wade stepped in. "This one's mine, sweetkins."

Right on cue, it seemed, the music slowed right down. Kim sucked in what felt like the slowest, deepest breath she'd had in days.

"Tired?" Wade asked.

She started to nod her head, then changed it to a shake.

He laughed softly, and put his hands on her hips, tugging her closer to him. "Anyone would be exhausted after the show you just put on. Where did you learn to Charleston?"

Kim pulled away, but only slightly. "You recognized it? Did everyone else?" Because if they had, they'd be thinking she was the biggest geek on the planet.

He chuckled. "I don't think so. My grandma and

grandpops used to 'show us how it should be done' on occasions when they disapproved of the kind of dancing we juniors did." He glanced around the crowd. "I suspect half these kids haven't even heard of the Charleston."

"Phew," she murmured.

"So, what's your follow-up act? The tango?"

She tingled at the mention of the sensuous dance. "I learned a little salsa."

"Isn't that something you have on corn chips?"

About to correct him, she realized he was joking. She stuck out her tongue.

He took a step closer, his eyes riveted on her mouth. "Do that again."

She clamped her mouth shut, and he laughed. "Chicken." Then he kissed her anyway.

Oh, it was sweet. Kim couldn't help responding, right there on the dance floor. His lips were so firm, so strong... When he drew back, she sighed.

"That bad, huh?" he said.

"Terrible," she agreed. Naturally, he didn't believe her. He laughed.

"Hey, Kim." It was one of the guys she'd danced with. "We're getting in a round of tequila shots. Want one?"

Kim shuddered, remembering how she'd felt after just two glasses of wine the other night. "Thanks, but no."

"Then come and watch," the guy insisted. He whisked her away from Wade, and a minute later she was laughing and joking with the hard-drinking, hard-rocking crowd. She almost pinched herself. She was at a wild party, and she was as near as dammit to the life and soul.

CHAPTER TWELVE

BY THE TIME 1:00 A.M. rolled around, Wade had had enough of watching Kim partying. He kept an eye on her, and the second she yawned, he told her it was time to leave. She didn't argue.

Damn right she didn't argue, Wade thought, his irritation long past the simmering point, and now at a rolling boil. Didn't she know she was ill?

"What's wrong?" Kim asked as they entered the elevator at their hotel.

"Nothing." Then he changed his mind. "Nothing's wrong with *me*. I wasn't the one cavorting with one guy after another tonight."

"Cavorting?"

Okay, so it was an old-fashioned word, the kind his dad might have used if he'd lived long enough to protest about Wade's sisters' dates.

"Flirting," Wade amended. "Dancing, drinking…" Even he thought he sounded like an old-time Baptist minister. Kim laughed out loud.

"It was on my list," she said innocently. "I didn't have a choice."

He narrowed his eyes. "So you're saying that if something's on your list, you have to do it."

"Uh-huh." She spread her hands, helpless.

"Let me see that list again."

She pulled the now creased and tattered list out of her purse. Wade smoothed it out. He pulled a pen from his pocket.

"What are you doing?" Kim tried to grab the list, but he moved it beyond her reach. He crossed out one word, added two more. Then he handed it back to her.

Her gaze went straight to the alteration. She gasped, then looked at him. "Are you crazy?"

The elevator binged—they'd arrived at her floor. The doors slid open.

"It's on the list," he said. "You have to do it."

Kim gulped. Wade had crossed out the word *Date* from *Date a jock*. And replaced it with two words: *Sleep with*.

The satisfaction she'd taken in not having slept with him was in that instant shown to be a big fat lie. Truth was, it was the biggest regret of her life.

"Well?" he said, as they stopped outside her room.

"I feel," she said carefully, "as if we've been here before." Last time, she'd turned him down because she hadn't been honest about her health, then she'd had that minicollapse before she could confess the truth, which she still hadn't done.

His jaw jutted. "I still want you. More than ever."

He opened the door, and they went into her room.

"And you still want that crew chief job," she said as she stuck the card key in the holder on the wall. The room lights came up. "That's your number one priority."

He nodded. "I won't lie to you about that. I'm not looking for a serious relationship at this point."

Kim caught a glimpse of herself in the mirror on the

bathroom door. She looked exhausted. Wade wouldn't be looking for a relationship *ever* if he knew.

"Wade, the woman you want to sleep with…"

"That would be you." He dropped a quick kiss on her mouth.

"It's not the real me." Kim sat on the end of the bed she'd left her suitcase on. "The party tonight, the tattoo…none of the interesting things I've done since I met you are the real me."

He leaned against the shelving unit that held the TV. "You think those are the things that interest me about you?"

"Okay, you claim you find my big words sexy." She still didn't entirely believe that. "But, yeah, those are the most exciting things we've done together."

He shook his head. "When I think about having a good time with you, I think about your crazy theories about jocks. I think about steak dinners, and I think about a quiet cup of coffee during a break at the track. Most of all, I think about this." He crossed the few feet that separated them in an instant. With his forefinger, he tilted Kim's chin. He bent to kiss her, gently at first, then more insistently.

It was a couple of minutes before they surfaced.

"That's all very well," Kim said, "but—"

He put a finger to her lips. "I don't want you because you're a riot at parties," he said. "Or because you make me laugh when you're drunk. I just happen to like you— the real you—a lot, and I want to make love with you."

It wasn't a declaration of love, yet the words came from Wade's heart, Kim knew, and they moved her. But no matter what she'd said about wanting to take more emotional risks in her life, making love with Wade wasn't one of them.

There was a difference between risk and certain doom.

"No," she said. And this time, she wasn't even going to pretend she wasn't a chicken.

THE RACE AT RICHMOND was one of the most exciting in the NASCAR Sprint Cup Series schedule. This was the race that would finally determine the top twelve cars that would contend for the NASCAR Sprint Cup Series championship title.

Justin had a good chance—he was ninth in points. But several other drivers were clustered in the same range, so success was by no means guaranteed. That put the whole team, from Dixon and Isabel Rogers down to the lowliest gofer, on tenterhooks.

Wade was very happy with the setup of the No. 448 car. He and Hugo had worked better together than ever before, and the adjustments the guys had made were exactly right.

But in NASCAR, the second you think you've got everything right, fate comes up to bite you. Justin tangled briefly with Dean Grosso on the first lap and, just like that, lost fifteen places. Another tangle half an hour later sent him even farther back so he was off the lead lap.

Worse, a few laps later he radioed into the pits that the latest clash had damaged the car's steering. Quickly, Wade fired instructions at the over-the-wall crew.

"Come in now," Hugo ordered.

Justin slid into his pit, and the guys went to work.

Twenty seconds later, Justin pulled out again. Pretty damned good, given the work they'd had to do, Wade thought. He breathed a little easier and, seeing him, his men did the same.

"Nice work," Hugo told Wade.

It was unusual for Hugo to comment during the race—he usually waited until he had the big picture at the end of the night.

"Thanks," Wade said.

Hugo prepared to head back up atop the war wagon. "By the way," he said, "I know Dixon said he'd announce today who's got the new crew chief job, but with the third car up in the air while Turn-Rite Tools makes up its mind about what they're going to do with Justin, he's decided to hold off. No point appointing anyone to a job that might not exist."

"No problem." Wade figured the more time he had to impress Hugo, the better. And he hadn't got through Kim's list with her yet. A few more weeks wouldn't hurt.

ISABEL WOULD HAVE preferred Justin to have had a better start to the race at Richmond. But there was no denying his attempts to regain his place on the lead lap made for edge-of-the-seat viewing. The atmosphere in the Fulcrum Racing suite could have been cut with an acetylene torch.

Justin entered his third pit stop a lap down, then came out of it back on the lead lap.

"How'd he do that?" Clay demanded. He'd been at her side most of the race, occasionally holding her hand, always leaving her a hundred percent aware of his presence.

"It's called the lucky dog rule," she said. "The first of the one-lap-down drivers gets to rejoin the field at the end of the lead lap after a caution. Justin was the lucky dog this time."

Clay frowned. "He got something he didn't earn."

"Pretty much every guy out there earns it," Isabel said. "But only one can have it."

Two hours later, Justin finished third. Which meant he'd made it into the Chase for the NASCAR Sprint Cup—one of just twelve drivers eligible to win the series championship.

The tension broke in the suite: cheering and stomping broke out. Isabel ordered champagne to be opened—it looked good, even if most of the men would stick with their beers, and besides, Justin had a champagne house as an associate sponsor.

Clay caught her in his arms, kissed her briefly but hard. She'd dated him every night this week, so she should be used to his kisses by now. But each time, he thrilled her anew. She reminded herself she was dating him for the money he could offer Fulcrum Racing—she wasn't entitled to any kind of thrill. She wasn't proud of her methods, but the team was her first priority.

"How about we find somewhere a little more private?" Clay said.

"I just remembered—" she cast around, trying to recall what was next on her mile-long to-do list "—that Gordon Green is a vegetarian, and he might not realize there's bacon in the onion tart."

"Do him good, might put some hairs on his chest." Clay had little patience with vegetarians, teetotalers, meter maids and anyone else he considered out to spoil the fun of the general populace.

Much as his blunt intolerance irritated Isabel, she also enjoyed it—mainly because Clay was tender, protective and respectful toward her and she loved the contrast. She hadn't felt so special in a long time.

She should enjoy it while it lasted. In another couple of weeks, she and Clay would be history.

THE TUESDAY MORNING AFTER the race at New Hampshire, Hugo's usually impassive face was grim and set. He moved around the workshop fast, barking orders with none of his usual controlled restraint.

"We need to talk," Hugo said as soon as he realized Wade had arrived.

Something's happened to Kim. Every scrap of air vacated Wade's lungs, and his vision turned dark. "Tell me," he croaked.

"My office," Hugo said, and Wade followed him.

"There's been a possible sighting of Kim's mom," Hugo said as soon as Wade closed the door. "A guy I used to know was on vacation in Alaska recently. He saw my ad in the paper and e-mailed to say he saw a woman up there who might be Sylvie, working in a gift shop in Fairbanks—city right in the middle somewhere."

"That's great," Wade said mechanically, still trying to rein in the panic that had gripped him at the thought of Kim being ill.

"If she's in Alaska, that would explain why she hasn't seen my ads and come forward. I need to go up there." Hugo began stuffing papers into drawers willy-nilly, as if he meant *this minute.* "I don't know how long I'll be gone, but we'd better assume that for the next two races, you'll be Justin's crew chief."

Wade's heart thudded. Crew chief at Dover and Kansas City! The ultimate chance to prove himself.

Hugo frowned. "Rachel will take over as car chief. We've done most of the work for this weekend, so it's a matter of running with what we've got, tweaking where necessary. But next week, you and Justin will need to plan the strategy. I'll watch the races if I can, and I'll be a phone call away."

"I won't let you down," Wade said.

WADE TOLD KIM ABOUT his elevation to crew chief that night. Right after he took her to the movies and thoroughly satisfied her desire to make out in the back row. Only two items left to go on the list.

"That's fantastic." Back in her condo, she handed him a cup of coffee and sat down in the armchair opposite the couch where he sat. Wade would have liked her right next to him, but he sensed she needed space.

Earlier tonight, before they made out, she'd been unusually reticent—Wade guessed it was because she didn't like the thought of Hugo going after her mother.

Now, talking about Wade as acting crew chief obviously made her think about her father's mission, and she turned quiet again.

"I know you're not ready to face your mom after she left you," Wade said. "But if she's a match, and you can have the transplant…"

"Yeah, I know." She sipped her coffee. Wade wondered if she was still within her fluid limit for the day, but knew better than to ask her.

"Tell me about your plans as crew chief." She changed the subject. "Will Dad still have a job when he gets back?"

He grinned, and lightened the atmosphere for her sake. "I doubt I'll achieve total world domination in two weeks."

"I think it's a good sign Dad asked you to fill in for him. Rachel does, too—she's pretty upset."

He nodded. "Of course I'm sorry about Rachel. But this is every car chief's not-so-secret dream. Every practice, every race, a hundred ideas roll through your mind about what you'd do if you were in charge. In your head, every idea looks brilliant."

"Now you've got to pick the best," she said. "And it might not be that easy."

"Not as easy as it is in my mind, that's for sure."

"You can do it," she said.

"How do you know?" Maybe Hugo had been saying nice things about him.

She tapped her head. "You're forgetting my enormous brain."

He laughed. "How could I forget? Hugo told me just the other day that you're about to win the Nobel Prize."

"Shut up." She picked up the teaspoon she'd used to stir her coffee and aimed it at Wade. He put up a hand, caught it before it hit him on the head.

"Your right arm is really coming along," he said.

She sniffed. "You jocks are so easily impressed."

But she looked pleased.

She was wrong, though. Wade wasn't easily impressed. Not at all. Yet Kim had snuck to the top of the list of people he…respected. Liked. A lot. Maybe even more than liked.

Uh-oh. He didn't want to deal with that now. He had two races to clinch the crew chief job, and he wasn't going to waste his big chance.

"How's your sponsorship assessment going?" Isabel stretched her legs in front of her, and leaned back against the cushions of the couch in her formal living room. She always had Clay sit in this room if he came in after they went out for a meal, so she could remember their relationship was business, not personal.

It was the first time she'd mentioned the reason she and Clay were together. His arm tightened across her shoulders. He took a sip of his red wine. "Are you hoping to get out of the last week of our agreement?"

"Of course not." She tilted her head, kissed his chin. The fact was, she was dreading the race at Dover.

He took her wineglass, set it on the coffee table alongside his and pulled her into his arms. His kisses, Isabel thought before she drowned in the sensation, were like nothing she'd experienced. When Clay did something, he did it right.

When he released her, she sighed.

"You're worrying," he said, half amused, half annoyed. He put a space between them on the couch. "You're afraid you won't be able to run that third car."

"If you pull out," she said, "there won't be any reason for you and I to see each other."

"Are you trying to scare me into the sponsorship?" he said harshly. "Dangle the prospect that I'll never see you again?"

"No," she said, stung. As if she could scare him into anything! Clay had never hinted he felt anything for her beyond a raging physical attraction. She had zero power over him.

His hand squeezed her shoulder in what might have been an apology. "What do you see happening if Turn-

Rite continues to sponsor Justin?" he asked. "Would you and I continue like this?"

Although she hadn't been thinking about the team, her heart leaped at the thought he might continue the sponsorship. But it was the thought of continuing to see Clay that set her stomach fluttering. "You mean, like this, as in casual dating?"

"I wouldn't call this entirely casual."

She expected more candor from him, expected him to say exactly what he was thinking. Maybe it was time for her to indulge in some of that plain speaking he was so fond of. Isabel grabbed her red wine again, anchored herself to the glass. "I've done enough dating that goes on and on but never turns into something real," she said. "I want to get married, Clay."

He flinched, which wasn't a good sign. "Not necessarily to you," she said, though just saying the word *married* had conjured up a seductive picture of him and her in a couple of years' time, posing in Victory Lane at Homestead with their winning driver. "I don't love you yet, but I could. I don't want to fall in love with you if you're not going to love me back—the kind of love that'll last the rest of our lives."

It felt good to say what she wanted.

Clay opened his mouth, then closed it again. He looked down at his hands, the blunt fingers with their clean nails. Unlike her, he wouldn't talk just to fill the air, he'd wait until he knew what he wanted to say. She supposed it was to his credit that he hadn't run screaming from the room.

He flexed his left hand, then looked up. "I could do

this—you and me—for a very long time," he said. "I could want you and no one else."

She nodded. Wanting wasn't the same as loving, he knew that as well as she did.

"I think we could have a future, Izzy. But I'm past the hearts and flowers stage. I'm looking for something different in a marriage. Companionship, compatibility…a partnership."

He leaned forward. "The only woman I've loved was Beth, who needed me as much as she loved me. What I like about you—" Isabel tried not to notice he'd used that wishy-washy word *like* "—is that you have your own life. You wouldn't be waiting at home for me, fretting that I'm not paying you enough attention. *I* wouldn't be feeling guilty that I wasn't there for you. The kind of love you're talking about, that seems like more than either of us might be prepared to give."

Considering she didn't love him yet, it was surprising how his words hurt. "You sound like Hugo, like Brad," she said, "apologizing for not being the man I want."

"It's not like that," he said sharply. "I want to be with you, but I need to be honest about what I'm offering. You need to think hard about exactly what you're willing to give me, too." He smiled suddenly. "But I'll tell you what, if we were together—if we got married— we'd get to do this all the time."

He tugged her into his arms for a hot, hungry kiss. As it grew more intense, he eased her down onto the cushions.

Isabel dismissed the oddly empty feeling inside her and with her mouth, her tongue, told him she agreed it would be good to do a *lot* more of this.

KIM ARRIVED IN DOVER late Friday afternoon. The team was still working on the car, and in the hauler, Justin was watching a rerun of his last race at the track.

Kim watched Wade at work, observed his easy command and the respect he earned. His style was very different from Hugo's but if he made it to crew chief, she had no doubt he'd be every bit as good as her dad.

Wade saw her and immediately came over.

"Hail to the chief," she greeted him.

"A hail of rotten tomatoes, most likely," he said. "I've discovered that being crew chief isn't the way to win a popularity contest. Every man and his dog has an opinion on our race strategy and on the car. Telling them Hugo and Justin have already worked out the game plan doesn't cut much ice."

"You're not making any changes?"

"Minor tweaks," he said. "Justin qualified twentieth, which Hugo wasn't happy to hear. I told him we'll do some work on the suspension."

"Still want to be a crew chief?"

He gave her a look that said jocks didn't give up their ambition just because it wasn't easy. "As soon as I learn how to juggle a thousand things at once, I'll be fine." He raked a hand through his hair. "I might have to get a bit less patient with all the people who want to say their two cents' worth and keep me too preoccupied to actually make things happen."

Kim saw Clay Mortimer approaching the garage. The brash Turn-Rite Tools owner looked tired, yet at the same time energized. Kind of how Kim felt after an evening with Wade.

"WHERE THE HELL IS Isabel?" Clay asked Kim. He'd been in Canada on business, so he hadn't seen Isabel in over a week. They'd talked on the phone, but neither of them had been in a good space—that conversation about the future had pushed them to a decision stage neither of them was ready for. Clay had started trying to imagine a future without Izzy and found it was like trying to imagine Charlotte without a racetrack.

He glanced around the garage. Dammit, where was she? With Beth, he'd always known exactly where she was. Waiting for him.

He realized Kim looked taken aback, and he replayed what he'd said in his mind. Yeah, too abrupt again. For Izzy's sake, he was trying to make more conversational effort these days. He wasn't interested in the minutiae of other people's lives—apart from Izzy's, everything about her fascinated him—but that stuff mattered to her so he was willing to try.

"So, how are you doing?" he asked Kim. Had she always been this pallid?

"Fine, thanks."

He remembered Beth saying the same thing countless times in answer to that question. They'd both known she was lying, but what could either of them do?

"I haven't seen Isabel today," Kim said. "Did you try her cell?"

"Switched off." He shoved his hands in his pockets and asked Wade, "How's the car looking for the race?" He was happy to wait and be surprised on Sunday, but Izzy would want him to take an interest.

Wade gave him an answer with exactly the right amount of detail, then headed back to the team. Clay liked Wade. He was a smart guy who had good instincts. And since Isabel had said he was dating her best friend, that was a good thing.

"Are things serious between you and Wade?" he asked Kim, still thinking about the possibility of marrying Izzy.

Kim colored bright red and said a repressive, "No."

Now Clay remembered Izzy had only said they were "sort of" dating. He probably wasn't supposed to know. It was so damned hard to tell with women what was a secret and what wasn't.

Isabel's strict social etiquette would dictate that he drop the subject and move on to something harmless, such as what kind of shock absorber the team planned to race on Sunday. Instead, he said, "I know what it's like, trying to make a go of it when one of you is sick."

Kim looked horrified, and Clay had the uncomfortable feeling that maybe he wasn't supposed to know she was sick, either. What did she think he and Isabel talked about?

Anyway, now that she knew he knew, he might as well carry on. "My wife had a heart condition." He told Kim how weak Beth had been.

Maybe because he was hoping things would work out for him and Isabel, he wanted to give Kim hope, too. "My job took me on the road a lot, like Wade's does," he said. "It wasn't easy for either me or Beth knowing I couldn't always be there for her. But we made it work."

Kim looked less than inspired by his words. But at least Clay could tell Izzy he'd tried to make conversation.

"That might be your idea of a good marriage, but it's not mine," Kim said hesitantly. Twin red flags in her cheeks told him how uncomfortable she was with this conversation, but she obviously wanted to get something off her chest. "I've told Wade, as I imagine your wife told you, that I don't want to be a burden on any guy." She shook her head. "What a crock."

"My wife—" Clay began, filled with an urgent need to defend his marriage.

"I didn't mean you," Kim said, horrified. "I meant I've realized *I* want more. It's not about whether or not I'm a burden. I want a guy who'll never see being there for me as any kind of hardship."

She stopped, her mouth half-open, as if she'd just realized she was saying deeply personal things to her best friend's boyfriend. "I, um, have to go," she blurted. Then she hurried out of the garage.

Leaving Clay sucker-punched.

Kim was right, dammit. More importantly, Isabel was right, every word she'd said at that restaurant on their first dinner together.

Clay had been a terrible husband. He'd made one paltry effort to change his lifestyle for Beth, and had sabotaged it by being difficult to live with. Selfish, selfish, selfish.

To clear away the guilt, he tried being angry with Beth for not demanding more…but he had a sick feeling that her undemanding nature was one of the reasons he'd fallen in love with her. Building his business had been the most important thing in his life, and, ill or healthy, Beth would never have dared ask more of Clay than he wanted to give.

Clay flung out of the garage, ignoring Wade's good-bye, and walked rapidly away. He and his wife had been very different people. For the first time, it occurred to him that if she hadn't been ill, they would probably have drifted apart. There'd been times in those early years, Clay realized, when Beth had been well enough to travel with him, and she'd chosen not to.

Hell, lots of marriages broke down these days. Most of them, according to some experts. Who knew, if Clay married Isabel, it might not happen to them some day?

Pain slammed him in the gut, bringing him to a halt next to the chain-link fence that separated the garage area from the rest of the infield. How could he have been such a fool? He couldn't lose Isabel, not now, not ever.

He curled his fingers through the fence, held on tight. Dammit, what he felt for Isabel wasn't the cooler, pragmatic flipside of his love for Beth. It was bigger, bolder, hotter than anything he'd felt before. The kind of love he normally only saw in movies he didn't like. A love he didn't even believe in.

Just thinking about his Izzy set his heart and soul on fire. His Izzy. Yeah, that's what she had to be. None of that independence crap.

He couldn't stay for the race, couldn't see Izzy until he'd figured out how he would make this work. He pulled out his cell phone, redialed the last number. He reached Izzy's voice mail.

"I can't watch the race, I've gotta do—" he gestured vaguely, aware that of course she couldn't see him "—stuff. But I'll fly you home Sunday night, we need to talk."

CHAPTER THIRTEEN

THE MOMENT CLAY'S PLANE reached its cruising altitude on Sunday night, he retrieved a bottle of French champagne from the bar fridge and opened it.

"What's the occasion?" Isabel asked as she watched him pour the fizzing liquid into two flutes. She was fairly sure he didn't even like champagne, but he'd been distracted ever since she came on board, so maybe he'd forgotten.

He handed her a glass, tapped his own against it. "I have good news…and great news."

His grin was infectious, and Isabel found herself smiling, too. "Tell me the good news."

"Turn-Rite Tools will continue to sponsor Justin—in fact, we'll sign a new three-year deal."

"Clay!" She almost dropped her glass in her excitement. "That's wonderful. How did your people get the numbers to stack up so well?"

"They didn't."

Isabel stared. "Then how—"

"Running three cars next year is a big deal for you," he said. "To my mind it doesn't make a blind bit of difference where Fulcrum Racing sits in the NASCAR hierarchy, but it matters to you, so that's good enough for me."

"But what about the cardiac research?" Isabel's mind reeled as she tried to understand what was happening here. Dixon would be ecstatic.

"Turn-Rite Tools won't be used to fund it," he said. "My priorities are shifting."

"Shifting…where?"

He laughed. "I thought you'd never ask. Now it's time for the great news—I want us to get married."

She clutched the stem of her glass in both hands. "We talked about that last week." She still hadn't decided if she could live with the kind of marriage he was offering. And she still hadn't answered the question he'd put to her—what was she prepared to offer him?

"Forget what I said." He took her glass from her, set it on the table. Then to her surprise, he went down on one knee in front of her. "I love you, Izzy. I want you and me to get married and to have the whole shebang— the romance, the works. I want to be there for you, with you, for always."

She'd heard—and said—the equivalent of those words at her wedding, but no one had ever said them to her in such simple, forthright terms.

Isabel's arms and legs felt oddly stiff, and she wanted nothing more than to drag Clay to his feet.

"What about your work, and mine?" she said. "What about those priorities you said we had?"

Clay clambered to his feet, ran a hand over his head. "I've been thinking about this all weekend, and I've worked out how I can make some compromises. I'm willing to cut back on my business travel—cut it in half— and have one of my vice presidents stand in for me."

Isabel felt as if a silken web was drawing around her, holding her back from the glittering prize in front of her, from Fulcrum Racing's return to glory.

"When I do travel," Clay said, "I'll want you with me."

She let out a breath. "But I'd be back for the race each weekend, right?"

"Sure, sometimes. But other times, I might be away two, three weeks." He took her hands. "Izzy, we're both too serious about our jobs to make this work without making some up-front decisions about what's most important. Our marriage should be the most precious thing in our lives, and the way we prove that is by putting other things aside. I'll stay at home as much as I can, but I want you with me, all the time. No matter what's happening at some racetrack somewhere."

She felt her face close. "I can't quit the team."

"You don't have to quit." He let go of her hands, paced the few steps to the other side of plane. "You just have to miss some races, it's no big deal."

Which reminded her how little he knew her. Isabel said helplessly, "NASCAR is my life, and you're asking me to give up a chunk of it."

"Dammit, *I* want to be your life."

The ten feet between them suddenly felt like a million miles.

"For how long?" she demanded. "My last husband left me. If I hadn't had NASCAR, I would have fallen apart. Same with the breakup with Hugo."

He snorted. "That wasn't a breakup, it was a mercy killing."

"It hurt me," she said, though in all honesty she could barely remember what she'd felt for Hugo.

"If I marry you, it'll be for life," he said. "You don't need to hang on to NASCAR in case I leave you. Trust me."

Isabel pressed back into her seat, trying to stop the sensation that the world was reeling around her.

"Let's say I do trust you," she said. "You could die. Then what would I have?"

"This is crazy." Clay's roar filled the plane. "No matter how many races you go to, no matter how many cars you run, you can't bring your parents back, you can't get your marriage back." He dropped his voice. "Isabel, you can't bring your baby back."

Isabel gasped. He'd cut to the heart of all her pain, to the loss that mattered most. She blinked away tears, folded her emotions in on themselves.

"I'm fond of you, Clay," she said—and realized immediately that she'd hurt him with her word choice. "But if I have to choose between you and my life in NASCAR, I'll choose the world I've always known."

His face sagged and he turned away, his hand shielding his eyes.

"I don't want to hurt you," she said miserably. And realized she sounded just like the men who'd let her down. She tailed off. Clay was right, in some situations, less was more.

She let her silence speak: she and Clay were finished.

TURNED OUT THAT ASSURING Kim she'd be fine driving a stock car and watching her do it were two very different things. Wade had to try hard not to triple-check her helmet and harness in the passenger seat of the customized driving school race car at the Charlotte track on Monday. Instead, he watched the driving school instructor check them, and grudgingly conceded the guy did a good job.

They would be here at the track for about three hours, which was more time than Wade had available this week. But the compulsion to finish her list was stronger for him than it was for her, and he'd crammed the stock car driving school into his schedule.

Kim's first few laps, the instructor drove. Wade knew the guy would be demonstrating the car, showing her the pattern of the stick shift and explaining the safety features. She'd already had the talk about how to master the track driving line, where to put her foot on the gas and where to lift it. All she had to do now was drive the thing herself. Easy.

The car pulled back into pit road. Kim and the instructor climbed out of their windows. Now, Kim would take over the wheel. She took a bathroom break first, but Wade's concern that she might be unwell seemed unfounded. He eyed her bright eyes, her hair flattened by the helmet that somehow still managed to look great, the curve of her lips. She was having the time of her life.

Wade told himself not to worry as she gave him a thumbs-up.

She started on the track just the way he liked—cautiously. Wade grabbed a spare headset so he could listen to her.

"This banking is so cool," she said as she hit the twenty-four-degree banking that made it hard for a person to stand up in the turns, but which made race cars stick just right.

Wade grinned at her enthusiasm. Gradually, she picked up speed, but still kept it within reason. Wade started to breathe easier. At this rate, she'd be lucky to hit much over a hundred miles an hour by her last lap.

She hit 100 five laps from the end, and her maximum speed on that lap was 120.

"Slow down," Wade growled into his headset, waiting until she was on the straightaway so he didn't distract her.

She snorted into his ear, and put her foot to the floor.

"Kim," he warned, then shut up because she had to negotiate Turn One.

She had three more fast laps, her top speed edging up a little each time.

Then it was her last lap, thank goodness. On the frontstretch, she got to 140, and the heat around Wade's neck had him rubbing it in frustration. She made it through Turns One and Two, then got to 155 on the backstretch. "Tell her to slow down," he ordered the instructor.

The guy raised his eyebrows, but even he agreed she was getting carried away, because he said into his radio, "Ease off, Kim."

Naturally because that guy was giving the order, rather than Wade—who probably knew a heck of a lot more about the car—she complied.

But not soon enough.

She entered Turn Three high, then overcorrected with a wrench of the steering wheel that sent the back of the car fishtailing. A shriek came through the headset, just as the back of the car hit the wall in Turn Four, spinning the car 360 degrees, so the front was the next part to hit.

Wade saw it all in slow motion, heard the bang, the screech of tires, smelled the acrid burning smell of rubber.

Then, mercifully, the car stopped, skewed across the racetrack. Wade jumped into the tow truck that took off from the pit road.

Leaning forward, hunched over the dashboard, he saw the safety crew clustered around the car. But he couldn't see Kim's arm out the window, waving that she was okay. She might not have remembered to do that, of course. He prayed that was the reason.

Dammit, he should never have let her do this. If something happened to Kim... Hell! He pulled back from the dashboard, leaned back in the seat, shaken at the realization how much it would hurt him if anything happened to her. Somehow, she'd become a part of his life, a part of himself.

They'd reached the car, and Wade jumped out of the truck before it fully stopped, earning a yell from the driver. He got to the race car just as Kim's head and shoulders appeared through the window opening. Willing hands pulled her from the car.

"I'm fine," she said shakily. "I'm okay." She submitted to the examination of the paramedics, who agreed with her self-diagnosis.

"Thanks, guys." Kim shook hands with the crash crew, told everyone repeatedly that she was fine. Everyone except Wade, whose critical gaze she resolutely avoided.

All the while she pressed the soles of her boots into the warm, solid pavement, shifting her weight from foot to foot. Reminding herself she was, literally, still on planet Earth, still alive.

Dr. Peterson's direst predictions had never brought home her mortality the way hitting a wall at 150 miles an hour did.

At last, she couldn't avoid Wade any longer. "I guess it's time we left," she said to him.

He nodded, took her arm for the walk back to his car. She tried not to cling, but, darn it, she was weak from the shock. Wade didn't say a word all the way to the Mustang, nor as she buckled herself in, nor as they hit I-85 back to Charlotte.

Kim decided to seize the moral high ground. "I wasn't in any danger. That car had more safety features than a jumbo jet."

"You drove faster than you should have for your skill level, and you crashed. It could have been serious." His voice was a monotone, quiet.

He was seriously mad.

A few minutes later, she tried a change of subject. "How's your preparation going for Kansas next weekend?"

He didn't say anything. A minute later she rephrased the question, still to no response. She had to ask it a dozen different ways before he finally consented to answer, about a half hour later.

"I need to work better with the team this week," he said. "We pulled it together at Dover because Hugo had done all the planning. But I don't have his skill at getting the best out of every person on the team."

"Of course you do," she said.

He glanced sidelong at her. "You haven't seen me in the team meetings."

"I've seen you with your family. You're a born leader

and a problem-solver—I can't think of a better combination for a crew chief."

Silence. Then he said, "If you think flattery will make me forget your lunatic behavior in that stock car…"

"It's not flattery. Those guys know everything about that car. What they need is someone who can get the best out of them. You can do that."

He reached across, put his hand on her knee, sending heat through Kim's body. "You can be pretty inspiring yourself," he said.

He pulled up outside Booth Laboratories—she'd taken a half day off work for the driving school. "Are you sure you're up to going to work after your smash?"

"One hundred percent," she said, pushing her door open. "I get to sit around and do my dialysis for the next half hour anyway. It's like being on vacation."

He saw right through her flip words to the lingering shock that weighted her legs and made her reluctant to get out of the car. Reluctant to walk away from Wade. He ran a finger down her cheek. "Sweetkins, you are one gutsy lady."

If I'm gutsy, why am I so scared?

"I've never been so terrified in my life as I was when you hit that wall today," he said. His sudden honesty mirrored her own thoughts so closely that Kim reached out and clutched his hand. He kissed her knuckles. "I can't deny—" he uncurled her fingers, laced them between his "—that you matter to me a hell of a lot more than I want you to."

"Thanks." She frowned through her suspiciously watery smile. "I think."

He leaned across and kissed her mouth. Kim got out of the Mustang and walked into Booth Laboratories on cloud nine.

JUSTIN QUALIFIED FOR POLE position in Kansas—it didn't get any better than that.

"Congratulations," Kim told her cousin and Wade as they talked race strategy outside the hauler after practice on Saturday afternoon.

"Thanks, cuz." Justin tilted his bottle toward her.

"You get some of the credit," Wade said to Kim. "I took your suggestions to heart working with the team this week, and everything came together seamlessly."

"Oh, well…" She blushed under Justin's interested gaze. "I am a genius, you know."

Wade groaned. In a good way.

Kim smiled back at him, aware she had to get back to the hotel and rest. She'd arrived in Kansas feeling less than a hundred percent. Only about twenty percent, if she were honest. Every so often, her vision hazed, and it had her worried.

"How about dinner tonight?" Wade asked. "There's a great steakhouse in town."

Her stomach roiled. Kim put a hand to her middle. "I'm not hungry. I have some reading to do tonight. And you guys need to do a bit more male bonding. You should go out with the team."

He eventually agreed, and Kim headed out of the garage across to the hauler, where she'd left her purse. She found it, went out again, barely aware of what she was doing. Her mind raced. Wade had offered her a steak dinner, her favorite meal, and she'd felt sick.

What had Dr. Peterson said when he was telling her the signs of deterioration to look for? "A sudden distaste for red meat is a sign that your dialysis is losing its effectiveness."

Could this be the beginning of the end?

As Kim stepped out of the hauler, her knees buckled.

WADE SAW KIM COLLAPSE. He dropped the shock absorber he was holding, sprinted across the pavement between the hauler and the garage to reach her. Already a couple of guys were helping her up and her eyes were open. Wade shoved his way through, said curtly, "Leave her to me."

He saw the relief, the gladness on Kim's face when she heard his voice. Darned right she should be pleased, because he knew how to take care of her and he wasn't going to entrust her to anyone else.

Naturally she made a fuss when he picked her up in his arms…but not as much fuss as he'd have liked. And her pallor—hell, if she was any whiter, she'd be a ghost. The thought cut too close for comfort.

"Get an ambulance over here," Wade instructed Justin's PR rep, who was hovering anxiously. "Kim needs to get to the hospital." He thanked God for the ambulances that were ever-present at racetracks.

Rachel joined them and chafed Kim's hands as they waited, exchanging anxious glances with Wade. "I'll go with her to the hospital," she said.

"I'm going. You're standing in for me here." Wade quelled her protest with a fearsome glare. He saw the dawning realization in her eyes that his relationship with Kim went far deeper than anyone on the team realized.

Which, knowing Rachel, meant Justin would hear all about it the moment she got him alone. Too bad. He fired instructions to her about the race, in case he had to spend the weekend at the hospital. All the time, he held Kim in his arms, absorbed the labored nature of her breathing.

"Did you forget your dialysis?" he asked suddenly. He wanted to think this was a simple mistake, not a sign that she was worsening.

"Of course not." She shifted in his grasp, outraged that he'd suspect her of such basic incompetence. "Wade, I need to call Dr. Peterson."

She handed Rachel her purse, and Rachel found her cell phone. Kim pressed to speed-dial the doctor. The ensuing conversation was brief, but seemed to reassure her—which meant it reassured Wade, too.

"He'll call the hospital and brief the staff as soon as he knows which one we're going to," she told Wade.

Then, with a wail and flashing lights, the ambulance arrived.

WADE HANDED KIM THE TV remote, then brushed the hair off her forehead. He leaned against the edge of her hospital bed. "You don't get to do anything more strenuous than watch the race on the box, doctor's orders."

"Fine," she said meekly, as grateful as he was that the doctors here had been able to stabilize her, to get her back to near-normal, so fast. It had only been an hour since she'd been wheeled into the E.R.

She ignored the fact that although the numbers looked good, she didn't actually feel normal. There was a weakness, a sense of something gone from inside her. *Maybe this is the new normal.*

"You need to get back to the track," she told Wade.

He shot her an impatient look. "I'm not going anywhere."

Alarmed, she tried to scramble up. "You have to, you're the crew chief."

He pushed her back down. "I'm not leaving you here."

"They're just keeping me for observation," she protested. "You have to leave."

"It's just a car, Kim."

Wow.

"My father would fire you for that," she said happily.

He reached out, ran a finger down her cheek. "Sweetkins, we should call Hugo."

"No," she said instantly. "He'll only feel terrible that he's so far away." Hugo had called last night to say he would start back to Charlotte tomorrow. Telling him she was in hospital wouldn't get him here any faster.

"And he'll feel terrible if Justin has a bad race. Go to the track."

Wade merely folded his arms across his chest and looked up at the TV screen, where the NASCAR Nationwide Series race played.

About to scream with frustration, Kim had an idea. "Is your sister here? Is Sarah at the track?"

"I believe she and Brent are back on this week," he said resignedly.

An hour later, Kim had convinced the doctor to release her into the care of Wade's sister, who could observe her as well as any other nurse. Sarah would stay in Kim's hotel room with her tonight, and they would watch the race together from Justin's motor home.

"Promise you'll let me know if anything goes wrong," Wade said as he settled Kim on the bed in her room half an hour later.

"I promise," Kim said.

"Not you." He looked at his sister. "You promise."

Sarah saluted. "Nurse's honor." Then she said, "Wade, Brent's planning a trip home to his family for Thanksgiving, but he says he's not ready to invite me along. Can you ask him—"

"Sarah," Kim said sharply. Sarah and Wade looked at her in surprise.

"Your brother is under incredible pressure this weekend," she said. "Some of it's my fault. It's not his job to fix your love life. Either do it yourself or have this conversation with one of your sisters."

"But Wade—" Sarah began.

"Kim, it's okay," Wade said.

"It is *not* okay." Kim hauled herself up in the bed and glared at him. "You told me that everyone needs someone to protect them when the going gets tough. Right now, you need protecting, and I'm it." She flicked a glance at Sarah. "Got it?"

Wade's sister nodded. "Sorry, Wade," she mumbled.

Wade gave Kim a smile so tender, so pleased, she felt her heart soften. "If you don't leave here right now," she told him, "I'll have a relapse brought on by the stress of watching Justin lose this race."

Wade's smile widened until it was full of supreme jock confidence. "He won't lose."

CHAPTER FOURTEEN

TURN-RITE TOOLS WASN'T entertaining in the Fulcrum Racing suite in Kansas. It was the turn of the smaller, associate sponsors and their guests, all of them thrilled to be there.

Isabel should have been in her element—a bunch of dedicated NASCAR enthusiasts, all convinced that sponsoring Justin Murphy was the smartest use of their money.

And Clay's lawyers had sent over a proposed new sponsorship contract for Justin—she'd never doubted for a moment that he would keep his word on the deal, even though she'd rejected his marriage proposal. Dixon was in negotiations with a driver for the third car, and hoped to make an announcement at Charlotte in a couple of weeks' time. Of course, rumors had gotten out, and she and Dixon had received a steady stream of congratulatory calls from some of the best-known names in NASCAR.

Everything was perfect.

So why was Isabel pining for Clay's gruff voice, his strong arms, his sexy shaved head? She told herself it was because he was larger than life, so of course she noticed his absence. He'd given her an ultimatum, and she'd made the only possible decision.

With a smile, she answered a guest's question about the degree of banking on the Kansas track, then elaborated on the track's relatively short history as a NASCAR venue. All the while, right up until Justin passed the checkered flag in first place, the words played in her head.

I miss him.

"SWEETHEART." HUGO HUGGED Kim, his eyes brighter than they should be—that's what came of telling him about the "Kansas incident," as Kim thought of it. He shepherded her into the house where she'd grown up, through to the kitchen that served as its hub. "How are you feeling?"

"Much better." Kim took a potato chip from the bowl on the island and ate it, as if to prove her good health. "Honestly, I'm fine. The doctor said I can go back to work tomorrow."

"You need to take some time off," Hugo said. "You can stay here."

"How about you? Are you feeling jet-lagged?" she asked, eager to change the subject.

A wave of his hand dismissed jet lag as being for sissies. "I got in at midday, I'm fine."

"This dinner to celebrate Justin's win was a great idea," she said.

Hugo nodded. "He's really hitting his stride. And Wade and Rachel stepped up to their new responsibilities better than I could have hoped." He pulled a beer from the refrigerator. "The others are in the garden. I thought we'd grill steaks—your favorite."

Kim got a nasty taste in her mouth. "Thanks, Dad."

The late September afternoon sun was pleasantly warm, and they stood outside while Hugo cooked on the grill. Wade stood close to Kim, his arm brushing hers. Reminding her of the care he'd shown for her at Kansas.

With Rachel and Payton holding hands next to her, and Sophia and Justin engaged in a low-voiced conversation a few paces away, Kim felt as if she and Wade were the third couple here. They hadn't had a chance to follow up on that cryptic conversation they'd had after her stock car crash. She couldn't wait to find out exactly what "you matter to me a hell of a lot more than I want you" meant. Maybe later tonight…

It wasn't until Hugo was serving up that Kim tackled the elephant in the room—mainly to take her mind off the enormous slab of medium-rare porterhouse that her father had put on her plate.

"So, Dad, did you find her?" If the answer had been anything but no, he'd have said by now.

"It wasn't Sylvie." Hugo passed plates around, directed them to the table on the deck. "Took me a hell of a long time to find the woman, and when I did, she didn't even look a lot like your mother. That buddy of mine has rocks in his head."

Kim's mouth tightened. "So it was a wasted trip."

"She'll come, if only she can somehow get to see the ads," Hugo assured her.

"More chance that my birth father will come," Kim muttered. "And he's dead." Under the table, Wade squeezed her knee comfortingly.

"We don't know that," Hugo said unexpectedly.

Kim stared.

"Your mother said he died, but obviously she had things…worrying her."

A euphemism for *She didn't want to stay with her family.*

"I wonder if maybe your birth father was violent, or a criminal, if he was chasing her, and that's why she left. She left you because you'd be safer with me."

It was a tantalizing thought, a seductive explanation.

"You have no evidence to support that." Kim didn't want Hugo finding another villain, when the fault lay squarely with her mother.

They'd moved on to store-bought cheesecake when Hugo said to Kim, "We need to find another way to get you a transplant."

"There isn't another way. Short of finding someone with my blood type and killing them."

Hugo actually looked interested.

"Dad, I was joking!"

Hugo wiped his mouth with his napkin, then balled it up in an abrupt, angry movement.

"You need to *stop* joking," he said. "I'm fed up with you not telling me what's going on. Do you think it's easy, seeing you look worse and worse each week? Knowing that anytime now, my daughter's need for a transplant might become urgent, but when it does I'll likely be the last person to know about it? Do you think it's a piece of cake not worrying about the fact that your blood type is so rare—"

"Dad," Kim protested. Beside her, Wade stiffened.

"That the odds of you getting that transplant are virtually zilch? You will tell me right now, young lady, exactly what Dr. Peterson has said about your condition, and if I decide it's bad enough, you will move in here, and you won't leave until you get that transplant or go out in a box!"

Rachel, Payton, Justin and Sophia sat shell-shocked at Hugo's outburst.

Wade pushed his chair back, got to his feet. "Is it true?" he demanded.

Kim buried her face in her hands, but he was having no more hiding. He pulled her hands away. "Kim? Is it true that your blood type is so rare you won't get a transplant?"

"No one can say that. I could get a transplant any day," she prevaricated, "and until I do, I'm going to hang in there."

"How rare?" Wade said ominously.

"There are other people who have it."

"One percent of the population," Hugo said. "There's virtually no chance of a donor organ coming from an accident victim or the like. We need a live donor."

"Why the hell didn't you tell me?" Shock raised Wade's voice.

"I don't have to tell every person I meet my full medical history."

"You're going to die!" he shouted.

"The hell I am," she snapped.

"Tell me—and your father—how soon you need the transplant."

Kim froze, knowing this was the moment of truth. The silence seethed, but no one broke it.

"I need it now," she said. "Before the race at Indy Dr. Peterson told me it was urgent, and things have been going downhill—slowly—since then."

Saying it out loud, she grasped the enormity of it for the first time, and began to shake.

Which had the positive of spin-off of redirecting her father's anger away from her and on to Wade.

"Stay out of this, Abraham," Hugo barked. "You're upsetting her."

Wade rounded on Hugo. "*You* stay out of it. You know damn well you should have told me about her blood type, that she's not going to get a transplant."

"Why should he—" Kim began.

"You lied to me," Wade said furiously to Hugo, "and you let me lie to Kim, which I would never have done if I'd known how vulnerable she was."

The words reverberated in Kim's head. "When... when did you lie to me?"

Wade let out a long breath and spoke more quietly. "Your father asked me to spend some time with you, to keep him informed about your health."

Rachel uttered a little "oooh" of consternation. Justin and Sophia exchanged worried looks.

"No." Kim grabbed the edge of the table. "Dad, you didn't."

But her father's sheepish expression told the truth. "I had to," he said. "How else could I find out? You're so damn secretive…"

"She's so damn *scared*," Wade corrected. "Can't you see, Hugo, Kim doesn't tell you anything because although she knows you'll protect her forever, she's not certain you love her?"

Hugo's face turned beet-red with anger. "Don't you lecture me about my daughter," he roared. "Of course I love her. I'd give my life for her."

"Then tell her," Wade said. "Don't make her feel as if she's just another item on the long list of Hugo Murphy's responsibilities. Tell her you love her."

Wade's confrontational attitude pushed Hugo beyond rage. He turned to Kim. "I love you," he yelled. "I love you more than anyone else in the world. You're my daughter, the best daughter a guy could have. And if you die, if you dare leave me, I don't—" His voice broke, and he finished in a whisper, "I don't know what I'll do."

"Oh, Daddy." Tears streamed down Kim's cheeks. She pushed back her chair, flew around the table, threw herself into his arms. "I'm sorry, I'm an idiot and a jerk. I love you so much."

She melted into his warm embrace, and for a few minutes became the child she'd never been, absorbed her father's pain, shared hers with him. Their tears melded in a shaking, heaving mess that made her happier than she'd ever been in her life.

When she and Hugo pulled themselves together, her cousins and their partners had gone. Wade was still there, standing several feet away, staring at the sunset. Waiting.

Kim extricated herself from Hugo's embrace with a kiss, and went to Wade. "So you asked me out because Dad told you to?" Hugo might be off the hook, but Wade certainly wasn't. "That's why you did all those things on the list? Dated me, made out with me?"

"Made out?" Hugo expostulated. "I thought he was building your shelves."

"Well?" she asked Wade. "What happened to wanting the 'real' me? All those things you said m-mattered to you?"

She stopped talking because if she let any more words out the tears would flow with them.

All those weeks of thinking Wade had chosen to be with her—believing he thought she was special, lovable...starting to believe she was the kind of woman who could be important, *necessary* to a man like him... All lies. Kim wrapped her arms across her stomach, trying to staunch the pain.

Wade's face was pale beneath his tan, but he came out fighting. "You don't come out of this squeaky clean. You asked me to dinner purely because you wanted to date a jock."

Kim ignored her father's horrified gasp. "You *jerk*." Dammit, the tears came out. "You knew I...I cared for you, and all along you were spying on me, reporting back to Dad."

She caught her breath, as all the pieces fell into place. "It was about the crew chief job, wasn't it? You told me it mattered to you more than anything, and I was so stupid, it didn't occur to me you had an ulterior motive for seeing me."

So much for that brain of hers!

Wade rammed his hands into the pockets of his jeans. "Kim, you know I care for you. I'm sorry I lied. At the start, I thought you weren't that sick, and you were using me as much as I was using you. And, yes, it was about the crew chief job as much as anything. Then I wanted to help you."

She thought back over everything he'd said. The words he'd used, and it only got worse. "You felt sorry for me," she said stonily. "You thought I needed protection."

"For a while," he agreed. "But you know it's more than that now."

"Really?" she said. "What is it, Wade? What exactly is it?"

"You lied to me, too, every step of the way," he said. "You didn't tell me the truth about your illness, didn't give me a chance to make a choice based on the facts."

He hadn't answered her question—he couldn't produce the words she needed to hear from him. The constriction in her chest, the blackness in her heart, told Kim she cared more for Wade than she'd ever wanted or intended. She'd fallen in love with the cheating, lying jock. *I love him.*

Yes, she'd lied, too. But when she'd kissed him, it had been because she wanted to, not because it might help her get a promotion.

Kim turned her back on him, clenched her eyes shut, put all her effort into producing calm, flat words. "You're dumped," she said. "Which means I've finished my list. Now you need to leave."

RACING AT CHARLOTTE WAS in theory more relaxed for the teams than racing anywhere else. Since most of the teams were based in the vicinity, the teams had more time to prepare the cars, because they didn't have to travel. Everyone had the same advantage, but teams couldn't help thinking they'd make better use of it than their opponents, which meant an optimistic mood prevailed.

But not in Wade's mind. He stood in the pits at Charlotte, watching the cars circle the track ahead of the green flag, and admitted to himself that the pain of not being with Kim was worse than the pain of being with her and knowing the truth. Since that night at Hugo's place nearly two weeks ago, Wade's mind had raced with the implications of Kim's rare blood type: *she could die, she could die.* The refrain ran through his head now, not drowned out by the noise of forty-three NASCAR Sprint Cup Series race car engines, nor by the cheers of the crowd.

And still, he wanted to be with her.

He had no choice but to forgive her for the lie she'd told him. Could she do the same for him?

THE TENSION OF THE DAY was getting to Kim. Justin had been uncharacteristically nervous when he got into his car, and Hugo was worried. Amazingly, he'd told Kim that himself, rather than letting her divine it from his silences and his occasional comments.

Wade might have broken her heart, but he'd done her a favor with Hugo. For the first time in her life, Kim felt one hundred percent certain of his love.

Wade… *I'm not thinking about him.* Ironic that as she discovered her father's love was genuine, she'd learned Wade's attachment was fake. At best, a product of his overly protective nature, so much like her father's. At worst, a self-serving grab at a promotion.

A fine sweat broke out on Kim's brow, nothing to do with weather, and everything to do with the nausea she'd been battling since she got to the track. It had hit almost as soon as she'd finished her dialysis.

It was a bad sign that the dialysis helped less and less, for shorter and shorter periods.

Not wanting to worry her father right before the race—but knowing she would tell him afterward—she moved carefully through the garage, intent on making it to the hauler, where she could sit down. Maybe even lie down, if no one was in the office at the front.

"Kim." Wade's authoritative voice stopped her, but she didn't turn around. She hadn't spoken to him since that awful night.

He stepped in front of her. "You're not well, shall I get an ambulance?"

How the heck did he know? "I just need to sit down."

"You're walking so stiffly, you look as if you're about to shatter."

She would have argued, if not for a welling of nausea that threatened to escape. She clamped her lips together and glared.

She might have known that wouldn't deter him.

"Can you walk, or shall I carry you?"

Her dad would freak out to see Wade carrying her. "Walk," she managed to say through barely parted lips.

He grasped her elbow, and she leaned into him. "How about we head to Justin's motor home?" he said. "I know he brought it here for you to use."

"Hauler," she muttered.

He sighed, then beckoned to someone. His sister Sarah appeared on the other side of Kim.

"Tell Kim she needs to go to the motor home," Wade ordered.

One look at Kim, and Sarah didn't protest her brother's bossiness. She grabbed Kim's wrist and took her pulse. "He's right," she told Kim.

But Kim had the morbid sensation this might be the last NASCAR race she ever saw—she damned well wasn't going to miss it. She pulled out of Wade's grasp.

"Justin said he wants me here. He thinks I bring him

luck at Charlotte." Her voice was stronger, she was pleased to note. "I'll rest in the hauler, then I'll be back out here after the race starts."

"You okay, sweetie?" Great, her father had seen the commotion and come down from the war wagon.

"Wade wants me to go to Justin's motor home to watch the race," she told Hugo. "But I'm fine to stay here, I just need to rest up."

"Of course you should stay," Hugo said. "We'll all look after you."

His intention was honest and good…but Kim knew that once the green flag dropped, no one would have time for anything other than Justin and the No. 448 car.

Still, she'd got her own way. She ignored the hurt and worry in Wade's eyes, and headed with Sarah into the hauler.

CHAPTER FIFTEEN

HISTORICALLY, CHARLOTTE was Isabel's favorite track. Some people had a stronger attachment to Daytona, but for her, nowhere was the NASCAR heritage more apparent, more alive, than in Charlotte. Just breathing the air at the racetrack was akin to a dose of the oxygen that some drivers claimed gave them an extra edge in their fitness training.

Too bad she wasn't there breathing that rarefied air today.

Instead, as the green flag fell, as the cars began the ritual, frantic dance for position, she walked up Clay's front path and rang the doorbell.

He didn't answer on the first ring, so she pressed again. When the door opened, she realized he hadn't heard her over the roar of the race on TV. His jeans were old enough to be bordering on disreputable—was that the beginnings of a hole in one knee?—and his black T-shirt bore the name of a rock group that hadn't had a hit song in twenty years. He looked wonderful.

"Isabel." He blinked and ran a hand over his eyes as if he wasn't sure it was her. "Why aren't you at the race?"

He hadn't invited her in—typical of Clay to forget

basic social niceties—so she walked past him into the house. The race played on the widescreen TV in the living room; she resisted the temptation to search for Justin's orange car among the pack.

"I quit my job," she announced.

"You *what?*" Clay grabbed the remote off the back of the couch and turned off the TV.

"I quit the hostess side of the job," she amended. "I told Dixon I'll stay on as sponsor liaison. He was most relieved—Justin has a very difficult sponsor who needs my touch."

A smile broke out on Clay's rugged face. He took her hands in his, caressed her palms with his thumbs. "He definitely needs your touch," he agreed.

She stepped closer to him. "But I can't do the hostess job, since I probably won't make some of the races next year."

She loved the way his eyes lit up. "Why is that?" he asked.

"I may be traveling," she said, "with my husband."

He obviously got the same kick out of the word that she did—he laughed out loud as he tugged her hard against him. She spread her hands on the broad expanse of his chest. "For every dumb thing you've said, I've been twice as stupid," she said. "I'm so sorry I hurt you. The last two weeks I've had everything I thought I wanted, and I've never felt so alone in my life."

He pressed kisses to her forehead, her nose, along the line of her jaw. "Izzy, my beautiful Izzy, you'll never be alone again." He pulled away. "Well, maybe when you go to the bathroom."

She laughed. She loved laughing with him. The

thought reminded her of the words she hadn't said. "I love you, Clay."

He took her mouth in a long, passionate kiss that left them both shaking.

"Darling, you don't have to give up your job," he said. "I wanted us to make some kind of statement, but I don't want to take you away from your world. We'll make it work."

She kissed him. "It's fine, truly. I'll still be involved in the day-to-day decisions. It means I'll enjoy the races I attend even more. Just promise you'll get me to every race we can, and that you'll be watching right alongside me."

"I promise," he said roughly. "I love you, Isabel."

He didn't need to say it—the love shining in his eyes made what she was giving up seem very small. Inside her head, Isabel said a last goodbye to her parents, her marriage, her baby…and in Clay's arms greeted the promise of a new life.

JUSTIN'S RACE DIDN'T GET off to a great start. The car was loose on the early laps, and he dropped back several places. Wade and his team fixed that up during the first pit stop, but just when Justin was starting to regain some ground, his left front tire blew out. That meant another pit stop, earlier than they'd have liked. Wade hoped they'd be able to compensate later in the race, but that wasn't always possible.

Despite his earlier nerves, Justin's driving was pretty good. He made up the lost lap and narrowly escaped a pileup that sucked in several other drivers who should have known better.

Maybe Kim did bring her cousin luck at Charlotte.

Wade's gaze stole to her, sitting up on the war wagon next to her dad. He hadn't seen her climb up—he suspected she'd deliberately timed her arrival for when he wasn't around—and his heart thumped faster at the thought of her climbing up there on her own, when she was feeling sick and probably dizzy as well.

Hugo was trying harder at his relationship with Kim, but he didn't see what Wade did.

Justin passed three rivals in quick succession, which had the guys cheering, and Kim leaning forward in her director's chair. Wade had to fight the urge to shout up an order for her to be careful.

Then Justin's voice came over the headset. "She's too hot."

The No. 448 car's engine was overheating.

Hugo said, "Can you keep her going without blowing up?"

Justin muttered something Wade didn't catch. Hugo said, "Take it easy for three more laps, and we'll hope for a caution to bring you in."

That was risky. If the caution didn't come, Justin would have lost several more places. Wade would have told him to get the car in here right now.

Hugo lucked out. There was a caution but not until Justin was nearing the end of his second lap. By then, he'd lost a couple of places.

Wade and the guys leaped into action, assessing the cause of the problem. It turned out that debris on the car's front grille was cutting off the air to the engine. All they could do was clear the debris, get plenty of air to the engine and wait valuable seconds for it to cool down. Then Justin was back on pit road, heading out to the track. Hugo gave Wade a thumbs-up, though Wade couldn't claim his guys had done anything special.

The rest of the race was mercifully uneventful, and Justin flew past the checkered flag in eighth position. Wade considered that an excellent finish under the circumstances.

He looked up at Kim, wanting to share his pleasure with her—and was just in time to see her slide down her seat.

He yelled at Hugo, who turned and saw what was happening. Hugo grabbed Kim.

Wade collared a NASCAR official, had the guy radio for an ambulance. All the while, he watched Hugo make his awkward descent of the war wagon, carrying Kim.

Hugo didn't argue about Wade going in the ambulance with Kim. Wade had never seen her looking so ill. The paramedic didn't look too happy about her condition, either. Wade filled in the medic on Kim's illness. "I can call her doctor," he offered. He retrieved Kim's cell phone from the pocket of her jeans, climbed into the front of the ambulance and found the number for Dr. Peterson. The doctor promised to meet them at the hospital.

Wade prayed all the way there.

By the time Hugo joined him at the hospital, Wade was just about crazy from waiting.

"How is she?" Hugo demanded.

"I'm expecting to hear from Dr. Peterson any minute."

In fact, it took another half hour. And when the doctor appeared, his face was grim.

"We got her through this crisis," he said, "but Kim is in a coma."

Wade's mouth had to work a few seconds before he found words. "Can you get her out of it?"

"She's badly dehydrated. We've got her on IV now, so she should come around in an hour or two." The doctor flipped a pen between his fingers. "But her condition is very serious. I've put her at the top of the transplant list. If she doesn't get a kidney very soon, we'll lose her."

An acid wash of fear coursed through Wade, peeling away the layers of self-protection so brutally, it was as if he were dying himself.

He couldn't lose Kim without losing all that was precious to him. *I love her.* He loved her for wonderful mind, her gorgeous body, her smart, sarcastic humor. He loved that she saw his vulnerability where no one else did, loved that she wanted to protect him from his demanding family. He loved her courage, that she'd conquered so many of her fears and gone beyond her own limitations. He could take a lesson from her in that, and in so many other things.

He needed a lifetime to learn from her.

The room turned blurry, but Wade could just make out Hugo peering at him, looking alarmed.

Ah, hell, I'm crying.

Disgusted, Wade knuckled the moisture from his eyes. Now he could never call Sarah's boyfriend a poor sap again. Even Hugo, though clearly upset, was restricting himself to a couple of loud, manly sniffs.

"I'll call you as soon as she wakes up," Dr. Peterson said sympathetically.

Wade shook his head. "I'm not leaving." His voice was steady, thank goodness. "Can I sit with her?"

The doctor nodded. "Of course. We can't be sure she'll know you're there, but she might."

Wade turned to Hugo. "Do you mind if I stay?"

"Of course I do," Hugo growled. "But given the mood she's been in since she dumped you, you'd better. Do you think there's any chance that famous charm of yours can put this right?"

"It will," Wade said. "I won't give her a choice—she has to take me back."

"That's the way," Hugo said. He and Wade shared a complicit handshake, then they both burst into slightly overwrought laughter. As if either of them could make Kim do something she didn't want to!

KIM WAS AWARE FIRST of the scent of disinfectant and boiled food. Then voices, far away. Then a familiar hum and beep of hospital machinery. Then strong fingers wrapped around hers.

Wade.

She tried to open her eyes, but her lids didn't move. She tried again, put all her strength into it, and this time, she succeeded.

She was in the hospital. Wade sat in the chair beside her, his gaze fixed on her hand in his. She flexed her fingers and wanted to smile at the startled jerk of his head as he looked at her.

"You're awake."

She'd never heard anyone sound so glad. Had she been that ill?

Talking seemed too difficult, so she tried conveying the question with her eyes.

Wade got it. "You need that transplant, sweetkins, and you need it now. The good news is, you're top of the list."

The bad news was still that she was a near-impossible match.

"Kim." Wade's grip on her hand tightened. "When you collapsed today, I realized a few things that I should have seen a whole lot sooner."

It took her a while to respond. "What…things?" The words were barely more than a breath.

He grinned. "I thought you'd never ask." The light in his eyes was so tender, her heart rate picked up. "I love you. I've loved you for weeks, maybe even since I first met you."

Her heart sang, every cloud on her horizon lifted. It took all her strength to confine her response to a skeptical sound. Because he'd hurt her, and she couldn't quite believe him.

"Yeah, I was an idiot," he agreed. "I lied to you and I was so pigheaded, I couldn't admit how I felt, not even to myself."

"Always were pigheaded," she managed to say.

He laughed. "You bet, sweetkins, and much as I'll try to change that, I can't guarantee it. But I can guarantee that if you'll marry me, I'll do everything I can to make you happy, and you'll never doubt my love for the rest of our lives."

Kim's rising joy was doused by those words—*for the rest of our lives.* There wouldn't be any "rest" unless something dramatic happened.

He shook her hand. "Tell me you love me, too."

"I—" She couldn't say it. Couldn't say the words that would tie him to her—how could she ask that of him?

"I can't marry you," she whispered, "when I might die."

He flinched. "You'll hurt me more by not marrying me. I'm being selfish, Kim. This marriage is for me. Sweetkins, I love you so much."

It was almost too much to resist. Her love over-flowed, so full and bounteous that she could barely contain the words.

She drew in a breath, and with it the last vestiges of willpower. "Let's…let's just take this one day at a time."

"Dammit, Kim, you're too sick for me to get mad at you, but lucky for you, I know you love me." Wade paced around to the other side of the bed. "I'm not going to let you—"

He broke off as the door opened and Hugo walked in.

"Kim, honey." Her father looked ashen, almost a hospital case himself.

Automatically she said, "I'm fine, Dad." But she couldn't stop the tears that leaked out of the corners of her eyes at the sight of his obvious grief.

Hugo said roughly, "Kimmy, we both know I haven't said this enough, but I love you."

He hadn't called her Kimmy in years. It made her cry harder. Darn it, she must be in bad shape if everyone felt they needed to tell her they loved her. She pushed away the shard of fear that stabbed her, concentrated on enjoying the knowledge of how loved she was. "I love you, too, Dad. No one could have been a better father to me."

Hugo leaned over, kissed her, then scooped her forward and cradled her against his chest.

Oh, damn, she really was dying.

When Hugo released her, she turned to Wade—he grabbed her hand, held on tight. She had so much to say to him…but she couldn't say it. Couldn't tell him now how much she loved him, then hurt him so badly by leaving him.

Hugo's sigh was an acknowledgment that although he might be the best dad in the world, he no longer held the number one place in Kim's heart.

"I have some good news," he said. "Wade, I'm going to recommend you for the crew chief job for Fulcrum's new cup car next season."

Wade frowned.

"This isn't about the fact that you're making out with my daughter," Hugo said. "You know damn well I wouldn't hesitate to fire your sorry behind if I thought you weren't up to your job. You showed me what you were capable of at Dover and Kansas. You deserve it."

Wade squeezed Kim's hand. "I appreciate the offer, but, fact is, Hugo, I'm not sure I want the extra responsibility. When we get Kim out of here, she's going to need care. I want to spend as much time with her as possible."

"No way!" Kim found the strength to protest.

"You don't get to argue," Wade said. "I love you, and I'm not going away just because you have some dumb idea about it not being fair on me for us to be together."

"Wade, I can't marry you," Kim said weakly. Actually, she was having second thoughts. Knowing Wade loved her, seeing that he was willing to give up on his own dream in order to be with her, was powerfully seductive.

Should she tell him yes, she would marry him?

Before she could decide, Dr. Peterson entered the room. "Time you left," he told Wade and Hugo. "Kim needs her rest."

Reluctantly, they departed. The way they vied for her attention in their farewells made her laugh.

And if she could still laugh, she must be doing okay. Right?

WADE DIDN'T GO BACK to work that day. He had some things to do, and he couldn't leave them too long—or it might be too late.

When he arrived in Kim's hospital room the next morning, he felt as if he'd wandered into the Charlotte airport during a snowstorm.

Hugo was there, with Justin, Sophia, Rachel and Payton. Isabel and Clay stood at the other side of the bed, their hands linked. Dr. Peterson and another doctor were chatting to Kim. The room was abuzz with conversation.

Damn, his timing stank. Wade didn't want to say what he had to say in front of a crowd.

Kim saw him, and her mouth widened in a breathtaking smile, giving him the impetus he needed. He wasn't going to waste another second.

He strode to the bed and announced, "One day at a time isn't going to work."

"Why not?" She sounded stronger than she had yesterday. Around them, a hush fell.

"For a woman with a brain the size of Texas, you can be pretty dense," he said. "You should know I can't be happy with less than all of you, for all the time you've got. You love me, and I know you won't refuse to make me happy."

Wade unsnapped his jeans. The whole room froze. He lowered the jeans on his right hip, just enough for Kim to see.

She gasped, clapped a hand to her mouth and made a stifled sound.

"That's right, sweetkins." Wade eyed the tattoo on his hip with some pride. He had the other half of Kim's heart right there...and he planned to secure her heart for real right now. "You and I belong together, and I have the tattoo to prove it."

He restored his jeans to their rightful position, and pulled a folded sheet of paper from his pocket. He handed it to Kim. "I wrote you a list—it's to replace the other one."

Bemused, she took it from him.

"I don't care which of your multiple personalities does these things," he said. "I love the chickenhearted, nerdy Kim Murphy, and I love the gutsy party queen Kim Murphy. You decide who you want to be, and then we can get on with our lives."

Kim unfolded the sheet and read aloud. "'Four Things to Do Before I Die.'"

"Hey," Hugo said, outraged. Kim waved him away.

"'Number one, sleep with a jock…for the rest of my life,'" she read.

That produced gasps from around the room.

Wade had a sudden uneasy presentiment. "Uh, you don't need to read it aloud," he said. "It's between you and me."

Kim was grinning. Either she didn't hear him, or she was determined to make him suffer. Ah, well, he deserved it.

"Number two, marry a jock."

Someone, it might have been Isabel, sighed.

"Number three, have kids with a jock." Kim's face glowed. "Oh, Wade, I can't wait!" She dropped her gaze to the last item on the list. "Number four…"

Wade blenched. No way could she read that out loud, not without Hugo taking the law into his own hands and shooting Wade.

Kim blushed furiously, delightfully, and folded the list. Her eyes met Wade's. "Mmm, yes, please."

Wade couldn't wait any longer. He pulled her into a passionate embrace, kissed her with all the love he possessed—and knew she gave him exactly the same in return.

At last he broke away. "So it's settled," he said, determined to pin her down before she changed her mind. "We're getting married."

She nodded. "After I get my transplant."

Frustration bit. "No way, Kim. I'm not prepared to wait."

"You don't have to." Her voice shook with hope and happiness. "Dr. Peterson found a donor. They're still running tests, but it looks as if we'll get the go-ahead."

"What?" Wade glanced at the doctor, who nodded. Wade realized this was why everyone was here.

"I tried to call you," she said. "Your voice mail picked up. But I knew you'd get here before I went into surgery." She tugged him down to her. "Your list was incomplete," she said. "I want to add something else."

He kissed her. "Anything."

"Number five," she said on a sigh of contentment. "Live happily ever after with a jock."

"You got yourself a deal," he said, and kissed her again.

* * * * *

For more thrill-a-minute romances set against the exciting backdrop of the NASCAR world, don't miss: TAILSPIN by Michele Dunaway. Available in September. For a sneak peek, just turn the page!

"I LIKE YOU. I LIKE being with you. But at my age and in my circumstances, I have to be up-front and lay my cards on the table. I have a daughter to worry about. Unlike my ex-wife, I've tried not to have a series of revolving-door relationships. I don't want Mandy to get attached to people in my life only to have them disappear when the fun's gone. I've never introduced her to any of the women I've dated."

Terri sat back against her chair. "Whoa. I didn't see that coming."

Max gave her a wistful smile. "Sorry. Now you know why I don't date much. I usually get about this far and blow it."

She mulled over his words for a moment, putting herself in his shoes. Max had a depth to him that was as refreshing as it was petrifying. However, she didn't want to walk away from him yet.

"No, you didn't ruin anything," Terri said finally. "I appreciate candor. I like your being up-front. It's a nice change from players who think life's only a big game. I may like to be carefree, but I'm not frivolous. I don't do casual."

"I'm not a party animal. I had to leave that life behind when Mandy came along," Max said.

"I'm still able to pick up and go. I guess that makes us opposites." She paused and studied him. She liked the way his eyebrows arched, and the way the lights danced off his dark hair. He was extremely handsome. "Do you think that's why we're attracted to each other? Because we're so different?"

"Perhaps," Max conceded. "I admit to not having a clue. But I don't want to stop seeing you. I sense something between us."

Terri sighed. "I do, too. But I'm not here because of the physical."

"Ah, good to know you want me for my mind." He faked a short laugh.

"Not that I don't want other things," Terri said quickly, deciding to match his honesty with some of her own. "Your body does things to mine. I get around you and short-circuit."

"Likewise," Max admitted.

"So Bristol?" Terri asked.

"I can tell you yes or no tomorrow," Max said.

He put his fingers on the carryout box and Terri gestured to the food. "As much as I'm sure we'd both like to linger, we should probably get going. You have to work tomorrow and Mandy needs to eat."

"True, and Mandy probably would prefer her food to be somewhat hot," Max said with a small smile. He didn't move yet and instead said, "If nothing else and Bristol doesn't work out, let's do dinner again when I don't have to rush off. I would like to get to know you better."

"I'd like that," Terri replied. She wanted to find out where things with Max would lead. He was so wrong for her, but somehow, everything felt so right.

They left the restaurant, and he walked her to her rental car. "At least it's an SUV," he said.

"I have to buy something tomorrow. Something about my rental days running out."

"Rocksolid only gives you so long to purchase a new vehicle once they've given you a settlement check. Most insurance companies are like that," Max said.

"So I've learned," Terri said, unlocking the car using the wireless remote. "So how long would you give me?"

"How long do you want?" Max said. They were no longer talking about rental-car days, but rather relationship length.

Such a loaded question for a first date. But oddly, the answer that came to Terri's lips was *forever.*

Which was silly, for she'd never been a forever type of girl. The last time she'd faced any type of permanent commitment, she'd turned around, given Harry back his engagement ring and run away as fast as she could.

"Just tell me you'll give me a quick kiss good-night," she said instead, giving him the opening for something they both wanted.

He leaned toward her, entering her space. He towered over her and then, ever so gently, raised her chin with his fingers and brought his lips down to hers.

He tasted better than chocolate cake was Terri's last cognizant thought as his mouth explored hers. She reveled in the feel of him, the gentleness of his lips, the teasing of his tongue. Then he was pulling back, the August air cooler than the heat burning between them.

"I'll talk to you tomorrow," he said, stepping aside so Terri could climb into her car.

"Tomorrow," she echoed, and she wobbled slightly on

the low heels she'd worn, a concession to his height. She managed to get inside, crank the engine and put the car in Reverse. It was still early, and nightfall nowhere close.

She saw him clearly as he stood there, waiting and making sure she'd backed up safely. Then he waved and walked to his car, carryout bag in hand. As Terri drove away, both giddiness and doubt crept in. The kiss had knocked her socks off. She'd thought herself in love before, but hadn't been ready to give up her freedom.

So what had had her asking Max to Bristol? Max was Mr. Serious. She was Ms. Footloose and Fancy-Free. She had the sudden insight that she was already in way over her head.

REQUEST YOUR FREE BOOKS!

2 FREE NOVELS PLUS 2 FREE GIFTS!

SPECIAL EDITION®

Life, Love and Family!

YES! Please send me 2 FREE Silhouette Special Edition® novels and my 2 FREE gifts (gifts are worth about $10). After receiving them, if I don't wish to receive any more books, I can return the shipping statement marked "cancel." If I don't cancel, I will receive 6 brand-new novels every month and be billed just $4.24 per book in the U.S. or $4.99 per book in Canada, plus 25¢ shipping and handling per book and applicable taxes, if any*. That's a savings of at least 15% off the cover price! I understand that accepting the 2 free books and gifts places me under no obligation to buy anything. I can always return a shipment and cancel at any time. Even if I never buy another book from Silhouette, the two free books and gifts are mine to keep forever.

235 SDN EEYU 335 SDN EEY6

Name	(PLEASE PRINT)

Address		Apt. #

City	State/Prov.	Zip/Postal Code

Signature (if under 18, a parent or guardian must sign)

Mail to the **Silhouette Reader Service:**
IN U.S.A.: P.O. Box 1867, Buffalo, NY 14240-1867
IN CANADA: P.O. Box 609, Fort Erie, Ontario L2A 5X3

Not valid to current subscribers of Silhouette Special Edition books.

Want to try two free books from another line?
Call 1-800-873-8635 or visit www.morefreebooks.com.

* Terms and prices subject to change without notice. N.Y. residents add applicable sales tax. Canadian residents will be charged applicable provincial taxes and GST. Offer not valid in Quebec. This offer is limited to one order per household. All orders subject to approval. Credit or debit balances in a customer's account(s) may be offset by any other outstanding balance owed by or to the customer. Please allow 4 to 6 weeks for delivery. Offer available while quantities last.

Your Privacy: Silhouette is committed to protecting your privacy. Our Privacy Policy is available online at www.eHarlequin.com or upon request from the Reader Service. From time to time we make our lists of customers available to reputable third parties who may have a product or service of interest to you. If you would prefer we not share your name and address, please check here. ☐

SSE08R

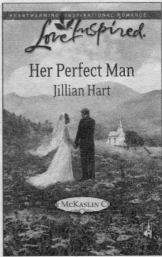